Making Corrections

A Time Travel Novel

Making Corrections

A Time Travel Novel

K. F. Whatley

Revised Edition
Published by KF Whatley
Zebulon, North Carolina USA

Making Corrections

A Time Travel Novel

Paperback ISBN: 978-1-7359260-0-1
e-book ISBN: 978-1-7359260-1-8

First published 2018 by KF Whatley
Revised (2nd) Edition published 2020 by KF Whatley

www.FictionWriterNC.com

For Frank and all the kiddos

*There are more things in heaven and earth, Horatio,
than are dreamt of in your philosophy.*
- Shakespeare (Hamlet)

Acknowledgements

Thank you to Donna, Corvi, Juli, Nicole, and Nadia for reading my drafts, and supporting my efforts. The encouragement of my family, friends, and writer-friends made publication of this fictional tale possible.

1 – Alone

Carrie Weathers had never believed in time travel. It was unproven, and probably impossible. Yet here she sat, reading the newspaper article on the time traveler over and over.

Her husband, Mig, had been gone six months, and she was having a bad week. There had been many hard days and bad weeks since Mig died, one painful moment stretching out to the next as she struggled to bear it.

As husband and wife, Mig and Carrie had worked as photographer and reporter, covering news and events in eastern North Carolina alongside strange news. Time travel hadn't been the strangest, nor the least likely.

Over the years, Mig photographed everyone from community leaders to bigfoot hunters while Carrie interviewed them. Heading home afterward, they had talked through their work — their "adventures" as they called them. Sometimes their conversations were serious, sometimes laughter-filled, usually with Mig talking as he drove and Carrie taking notes for the articles-to-be. They'd joked all the way home after meeting the time traveler.

Since Mig's death, Carrie had been working alone to keep the newspaper going; her hope to fulfill Mig's dream of building the newspaper he'd started into a regionally recognized name. Doing it *for him* motivated her. He'd been a good man, kind to all, and beloved by her, the children, and grandchildren. She thought that he deserved a legacy.

It had been a wonderful life. Their days had been spent working together, their evenings home with the kids or — after the youngest child went to college — the two of them hanging out. Their time together had been a blessing, and after Mig died, Carrie felt his absence around the clock.

Carrie had started the day looking through old photographs. That led her to reading some of her, and Mig's, newspaper articles and thinking of all the places they had been together, and the oddities they had seen, shared, and talked about. Reading through the newspapers, she cycled from mourning to joy and back again as each memory stirred.

Today she had paid special attention to the strange news articles. In the corner of her mind, she wished one of the supernatural-focused people they'd interviewed might be able to do what the doctors hadn't. She and Mig had given the ghost hunters and alien spotters the benefit of the doubt, covering them with the same respect as community leaders. *Why not apply that same faith in their abilities?*

No, she had countered. *He's gone, and nothing can undo his death. If only we'd found the cancer earlier, he could have beat it.*

Her mind taunted her with thoughts of life with Mig versus the painful days she faced without him, and she had kept reading.

At one point she had come across a photograph showing a group of self-proclaimed witches. They had been part of an autumn event and had told her and Mig of the powerful forces they commanded. *I wonder if they could help me*, she had thought, immediately telling herself, no, they couldn't be any help.

Still, she had looked the witches up online and found the coven website quickly. She thought about picking up the phone and calling them, then chided herself and leaned back. She couldn't contact the witches. Mig, and she, had believed in a benevolent God and putting good, positive energies into the world. She just didn't know enough about the witches' beliefs to be comfortable delving further into what they did.

Recognizing how crazy the idea was, Carrie had tossed the newspaper back in the file cabinet, wringing her hands as her grief swelled up. Finding a supernatural solution was a fool's errand, but that hadn't stopped her from continuing to search.

She had grown dispirited as the afternoon advanced. After a break to heat leftovers, and a short bout of crying when she had started to make lunch for two, she scanned more articles on their news site.

Then, a photo had caught Carrie's eye. She had swallowed the last bite of food and focused on it. Mig had taken it at a paranormal expo where a strange character named Peter Braggin had presented on the ethical boundaries of time travel. Carrie remembered that they had interviewed Mr. Braggin after his presentation.

They had spent about thirty minutes talking to the maniacal, mesmerizing Mr. Braggin, who extolled the virtues of time travel when used on a small scale.

On their way home after the expo, she and Mig had marveled at the odd tack Mr. Braggin had taken with his presentation. He hadn't talked about theoretical points of time travel, nor waxed on about science fiction's portrayal of it. He had focused on the ethics of it and shared how he viewed changes in history as acceptable or unacceptable. Most striking, though, was that he spoke of how time travel *should* be done properly — as if traveling through time was a normal thing to do.

Even though they'd met many speakers that day, they were both struck by Mr. Braggin's attitude. Carrie and Mig's conversation on the long drive home had included more than an hour of half-serious, half-joking review of that thirty-minutes with the time traveler. In the course of their joking, they had christened him "Spiky Hair Guy" and decided he'd made it the most fun they'd ever had covering an event.

Now, several years later and six months after losing Mig, Carrie sat curled up on the couch in Mig's battered bathrobe with the article in front of her. She twisted her pony-tailed hair absentmindedly, as she thought about Spiky Hair Guy and his time ethics.

Next to the article was a photo of Spiky Hair Guy with a backdrop of the event poster; the photograph's caption read, *Peter Braggin, Guest Speaker. Photo by Miguel Weathers.* She smirked as she remembered Mig describing Mr. Braggin's manner, "socially awkward doesn't quite cut it." That was between them, and not part of the article.

She wondered if there was even a remote chance that this quirky "expert" could be a genuine time traveler. Time travel was as impossible as any other crazy idea she'd considered, wasn't it? *Except maybe this scruffy scientist could go back in time,* she couldn't help but think.

Really, she chastised herself, *is this where I'm heading?*

She fluffed the bathrobe to cover her exposed foot, then sipped at her cooling coffee. Setting down the mug, she picked up her e-cigarette and vaped a little as she thought.

She didn't *really* believe in time travel. Yet, maybe as the bad days stretched on, she *needed* to believe life without Mig wasn't permanent.

As the light faded in the room, Carrie realized that the day was almost gone, and she'd accomplished little. She arose and went to the kitchen to refill her coffee mug. She stirred in milk, then absentmindedly stirred a second mug sitting next to the coffee maker. It was Mig's favorite mug, full but untouched.

Then, an idea bloomed in her mind. *I'll call the time traveler for an interview,* she thought. *At the very least, I'll write an article on Peter Braggin for the newspaper.* Having this logical, realistic idea pleased her. It didn't last long, wiped away seconds later as she dared to think, *Maybe, just maybe, he can do the impossible.*

The next morning, Carrie awoke early. Her first thought was the time traveler. She slid out of bed and went straight to her desk. From a drawer, Carrie pulled out one of her notebooks. She'd used dozens over the years as she reported on events and people. This particular notebook covered the month of the expo.

She flipped through until she found the pages containing her notes from their conversation with the time traveler. There were bullet points she'd used for the published article along with a few extra bits, including Mr. Braggin's phone number.

In the corner of the page was a caricature labeled "Spiky Hair Guy." It made her smile, and she wondered when Mig had added that doodle to her notebook.

The expo had been several hours away, but it had turned out that Mr. Braggin came from Hope Wells, the same town as Carrie and Mig. She hoped that he still lived there, as she dialed his phone number.

2 – The Interview

As Carrie navigated to Peter Braggin's address, the grandeur of the neighborhood surprised her. She wasn't sure what she had expected, but as she drove the houses seemed to get larger — far beyond the reach of a crazy man who gave lectures on time travel ethics.

Grant money, perhaps, she guessed, then dismissed the thought. She couldn't imagine someone was paying Spiky Hair Guy to study the ethics of time travel. *Family money? Maybe.*

She pulled up to his address, then turned into the empty driveway. It was wide and curved toward the side of the house. She parked and looked over the house's old stone facade. *Tudor,* she thought, then wondered if that was the correct name for the building style. With the stone along the front, it reminded her of a castle. There weren't turrets, but its roof had multiple peaks, and the colors of the stones gave it an almost medieval look.

Walking up the sidewalk, she noticed weeds among the paving stones. It made the house seem unkempt. *Just like Mr. Braggin.*

Carrie rapped lightly on the front door. Part of her wanted to leave. *Just get into the car and go home*, she thought. Instead, she stared at the front door's peeling paint and tarnished door knocker, waiting, her feet rooted to the porch.

Several days before when Carrie had called Mr. Braggin, she had explained her interest in writing an article and letting their readers know how his work was progressing. He had been polite but curt. She figured it was just Spiky Hair Guy being a stereotypical aloof scientist. *Socially awkward doesn't quite cut it*, she heard Mig say in her head.

Still, Mr. Braggin had agreed to meet with her, and now here she was at his front door. She wasn't backing out now.

Carrie had not mentioned to Mr. Braggin her desire to know if he *could* time travel or was all talk. *If* this guy was for real, then she would ask him to use time travel to save Mig from dying.

She wouldn't mention to Mr. Braggin, or anyone, that she had spent the weekend questioning what she should do, what's right and what's wrong. She'd gone to church Sunday morning, which had only increased her confusion. Mig's had been such a strong faith, while Carrie was always working to find hers. She wasn't sure if what she wanted to do was right. Mig had been her go-to when she wanted to discuss religious concepts, or faced a dilemma. Heading home from church, it was usually Carrie asking questions and Mig talking about scripture, his beliefs, and asking her questions in return. Now he wasn't here, and she worried she might be heading down a wrong path. In the end, her grief had driven her decision. Right or wrong, she needed to know if time travel offered a way to be with Mig again.

As she waited for Mr. Braggin to answer the door, she reached toward its peeling paint, then quickly withdrew her hand. The neglected door reminded her of the year that they'd bought their own home. It had needed paint, care, and fixing when she and Mig had moved in with the children. She thought of how they had worked together to make the house their own, and the memories stoked that now-familiar pain in her heart. So many ordinary objects triggered that pain. She shifted her thoughts to the present, steeled herself and focused on the door, waiting for it to open.

Carrie knocked again, this time harder. Finally, Mr. Braggin answered the door and gestured for Carrie to enter. Once he'd closed the door behind her, he led her down carpeted stairs and through a doorway into a panel-covered office. It was a long room, more 1970s than medieval, and at its far end a sliding door opened onto a patio beyond.

Spiky Hair Guy sat behind a broad desk, opposite Carrie, who sat down on a wooden chair with an aging velvet cushion. An unusual scent hung in the air; but, she couldn't place it.

His desk looked disheveled, just as he did, except while the room was casual, he seemed stern. His demeanor since he'd answered the door was gruff, and he wouldn't look at her.

"So, where would you like to begin?" he asked, though it sounded more like a statement than a question. Carrie wondered if his attitude was normal for him — he'd been talkative at the expo.

She figured she should stick to her plan and begin interviewing him. "When we, Mig and I, talked with you several years back," she started, "your focus was on the ethical use of time travel."

"Yes," he said. He stared away, looking out a large window at nothing. All there was to see was sky, and there were no clouds.

"Well," Carrie continued, "It's been a while since then, and I'd like to discuss how your work is going, and if you have any updates I might share with our readers."

"Yes. Sure." He stopped staring out the window but looked down at his shoes, still avoiding her gaze.

Carrie started to speak, then stopped herself. The silence drew out.

Finally, he said, "Mrs. Weathers, I was sorry to hear about Mr. Weathers' passing. You have my condolences."

"Thank you," she said quietly. Her eyes began to tear and she tilted her head in the hope of stopping them. She'd read somewhere that if you look up, your eyes will stop tearing. It kind of worked, and she wiped away the bit of water that had escaped, hoping Mr. Braggin hadn't seen. *I'm supposed to be professional,* she scolded herself.

He stood up quickly, startling her. Then he turned and began running his fingers along his bookshelf. Piles of papers alternated with books. He shuffled through them before sliding out a three-ring binder. Turning to sit at the desk again, for the first time, he looked directly at her.

"Mrs. Weathers, I'll be happy to go over some of my more recent work." He paused and looked at her intently. "I've been speaking on the increase in incidents with multiple victims in recent years. It's a grim topic, but you may be able to turn it into an interesting article for your paper." His eyes showed a sadness that seemed mismatched to his formal tone.

Keeping up appearances, Carrie spent the next twenty minutes asking questions and writing down Mr. Braggin's answers. Occasionally, he flipped through the binder and showed her papers he had published. She took notes, then asked him about his most recent lecture, which she'd seen mention of online.

"My latest lecture..." An expression drifted across his face and disappeared before she could interpret it. "Yes, I covered, theoretically, the potential misuse of time travel to adjust the timeline after multiple deaths. When you have a tragedy with dozens of people lost, there is more chance of unexpected ripples through time in attempting to reverse the event."

It struck Carrie that Mr. Braggin sounded more like a college professor than the fast-talking, socially-awkward man she and Mig had met. Carrie listened as he explained, lucidly, "In general, I focus on what *should* be corrected, not what *can* be, using the power of time travel. You and Mr. Weathers may have heard some of this before, but to provide you with more background for, ah, the purposes of your article," Mr. Braggin glanced at her, then away, "Why don't I start by telling you about my rules for using time travel?"

"That sounds helpful. Please do." Carrie didn't care where he started, as long as he kept talking. The more he shared, the better her chances of figuring him out.

3 – Rules and Roles

Peter Braggin cleared his throat, then said, "Time is a thing that must be treated with respect. One can't take lightly the decision to change history, even a small event." He paused, and his brow furrowed. His eyes cast down again and his lips thinned.

Carrie began to feel uncomfortable. His words seemed to speak directly to her desires.

He sighed and continued, "Correcting history has been my life's work, from early on, and I have a responsibility to choose carefully what I change. What I *allow* myself to change. I created my own set of rules, and while there is an aspect of luck involved, planning carefully within the bounds of my rules helps me control the outcome.

"I've adjusted my rules over time." A wry smile crossed his lips without reaching his eyes, "No pun intended."

Carrie thought that the bad pun was very intended but said nothing.

His gaze dropped again before he continued, "First off, I have a rule against using time travel to adjust life for those who have died very young. People have come to my door and asked me to bring back a baby they'd lost, and I don't consider changing the outcome for someone so young." He closed his eyes and sighed, "And believe me, people do not take it well when I refuse." Opening his eyes, he continued, "I see adjusting a short life as a major addition to their timeline. It's one thing to change recent events or tweak something minor that impacts the future, but quite another to give someone a long life who did not already have years along the timeline."

He doesn't sound like he's speaking hypothetically, Carrie thought.

He continued speaking about his next rule. "I won't help a person change the past so that they may *discover* something before their colleague discovers it, either. Nor will I change someone's life so that they can invest or hit the lottery to become wealthy. That may seem draconian, but that's one of my rules. It is a moral boundary I've set." He said the last firmly, as if cutting off a coming argument.

Carrie didn't think that was draconian at all. In fact, it pleased her to know he wasn't a fan of greed.

Peter coughed, and picked up a mug on his desk, taking a gulp. "I also have a rule that I will not help someone who wishes to change events in a time before they were born. It puts them and their family at risk." He shook his head as he set the mug down, inadvertently shaking liquid onto the desk. He blotted the spill with tissues and tossed them across the desk into a trash can.

"I will admit though," he said, looking slightly embarrassed, "that I have traveled to a time before I was born. But that was before *I* was setting the rules."

The emphasis of "I" in his statement puzzled Carrie. *What was going on before he set the rules? Was someone else involved?*

"I won't go back to assassinate a world leader. That rule is crucial. While it might seem a good thing for humanity, it affects too many lives. I'm comfortable causing small ripples, but I don't want to mess with what could result in a tsunami, regardless of the good it might do. The same is true of my recent work, if on a smaller scale. Do you understand what I mean?"

He looked at her quizzically, and Carrie knew he wanted to hear what she had to say. But she wanted to say, "Are you really able to time travel? Bring back my husband." She said neither of these. All she managed was a gurgling sound and a head nod.

He nodded back, more of a reflex than any type of acknowledgement, and went on. "Along the same lines, I will not travel to serve a military purpose. A few military types have shown up on my doorstep over the years, asking questions. I see them coming a mile away. It's a sense I have, for spotting people with ulterior motives. Nobody should use time travel as a weapon." He said this sternly, as if someone had asked him to do so.

"One man showed up in a black suit." He shook his head, "Others have come in disguise, but they don't fool me." He turned to her with wide and sincere eyes. "In fact, when dealing with military or government people who come to me, it is imperative that *I* fool *them*."

Carrie had taken no notes for a while, transfixed. Most of interest to her, as Mr. Braggin had described his rules, she zeroed in on the fact that bringing back Mig wouldn't break any of them. *If he could actually travel through time*, she thought.

He shrugged. "I'm going to be frank with you," Mr. Braggin's voice grew stronger, not commanding but solemn. "I play act as an artificial mad-scientist, an inept person, to screen visitors — for my own safety and as part of my role as protector of time travel capability. I am quite serious about my ability to travel through time, to help others within reason, and I necessarily cloak myself in a maniacal, artificial skin."

A sheep in wolf's clothing, she thought, reversing the proverb, *to protect himself from the wolves*.

"You and your husband saw one of my role-plays at the expo, and you saw a shade of it when you arrived. This allows me to find deserving people to help, or exhibit just enough crazy to keep the wrong people from taking too much interest."

Spiky Hair Guy, Carrie thought. "I think I understand," she said.

He nodded and continued, "If I get a bad feeling from one of my visitors, like they want to take over the world, maybe do some overthrowing, raping and pillaging," he shook his head, "then I pack on the crazy nice and tight."

Carrie wondered what *that* looked like. Spiky Hair Guy had been pretty bizarre. So had the curt man who'd opened his front door to her a short time ago.

"Micro expressions help me fool visitors, too. Those are brief facial expressions that happen naturally, and I've taught myself to use them intentionally. I've used them to falsely display fear and deception for the government-types who have come calling. They've read my expressions, listened to my ranting, and off they went."

He laughed, swiveling in his chair to face his office doorway. "One of those military guys who came by... well, he was out the door in ten minutes and never came back. Probably reported to his superiors that I was a nut. At least, that's what I hope."

Mr. Braggin picked up his coffee mug and took a swig. "Mrs. Weathers, my rules create boundaries for myself. I've been able to travel to help people's loved ones or fix a mistake, to re-do a conversation or an act, and know any repercussions will be reasonable."

Like traveling through time is a normal thing to do, she heard in her head. It was something Mig had said as they'd driven home from the expo.

Mr. Braggin suddenly stopped talking and stared at her. She returned his gaze, then found she couldn't break away from it. His eyes bored into her. One moment Mr. Braggin blended well with his messy, disorganized office. The next, he brushed his hair back with his hands and straightened, appearing taller in the chair. He leaned his arms on the desk top, hands clasped, and she watched as his eyes softened. *He knows why I'm here. And why wouldn't he? He just told me that he is very good at reading people.*

He finally released her from his gaze. "With that said, I believe there is no sense in either of us keeping up appearances, Mrs. Weathers. Let's get down to business." He leaned back in his chair, tapping his hand on his desk as if punctuating his statement. "You're not here about an article, or at least, not *just* an article. And, no, I am not the madman you and your husband thought me to be. Let's *really* talk."

"What?" was all Carrie could muster. He looked right into her eyes again, and she saw only compassion. Suddenly, she understood his curtness. *Did he know why I wanted to see him from the moment I called about this meeting? Or when I arrived?* It was apparent to her that he'd talked about having rules, and people not fooling him, for her benefit. She shivered.

Mr. Braggin continued, "There are more rules, and other considerations, but that's enough for you to understand the seriousness with which I approach time travel. My desire is to help people, and I carefully work to benefit good people while causing few ripples."

He turned to face her, "What's that saying about using gifts wisely?"

She heard a laugh escape her, although nothing was funny. "Do you mean, with great power comes great responsibility, from the Spider-Man movie?"

He emitted a brief "Humph," and looked down. "I think I had something more biblical in mind, maybe from *Romans*."

Carrie flushed at her pop culture reference, reflecting her low level of Bible knowledge.

She pressed on, "How many have you helped?"

He looked thoughtful for a moment. "Hundreds and hundreds." He paused, then chuckled. "Actually, with ripple effects, I haven't totaled how many people have been affected. I know that with each trip there were little corrections that helped, and nothing major went awry."

She looked him up and down. *How could he have helped many hundreds, when he looked like he was, at most, fifty?*

She dismissed that thought, but not before he offered, "Well, I'm older than I look. I don't age like I used to."

He continued talking, but for a moment she understood no words. Overwhelmed, her ears began ringing. She shook herself mentally, and without meaning to, shook visibly.

The time traveler gazed at her. "I trust you'll keep my secret, for your own good as well as mine."

"Why would you trust me?" Carrie blurted.

"We'll get to that," he said, rotating his chair, and looking out the window again.

Carrie could think of nothing to say, but she imagined Peter Braggin traveling through time, whatever that looked like, and then the world changed with Mig back in it.

He glanced at her, then back out the window. *Not out of the window, but at it*, she thought. Carrie waited, slowly absorbing what she'd heard so far.

4 – A Secret Room

"So, now that you know about me, know that I do not share the truth lightly," Peter said. "There's more you need to know, and to get to that, I need to show you my time machine," he held up his hands and put air-quotes around *time machine*. "It will be off the record, as you news people say, and you can't take photographs."

Carrie didn't want to expose Peter Braggin, time traveler, to the world. If he was willing to show her, she wanted to see it. Despite the grief and fog, she was not just Mig's wife, but a reporter, and the opportunity to gain knowledge of one of humanity's mysteries could not be turned down. She confirmed quickly, "Yes. Off the record."

He tapped his hand on the desk again. "Good." He pressed down on the armrests and hopped up from his chair, then motioned for her to follow him. He stepped to the wall behind his desk, pushed his hand against the trim, and a panel popped open, revealing a hidden room. He pulled the panel toward him, opening it wide, and Carrie followed him through the unexpected doorway.

My dining room is bigger, she thought. The room was small, at most 15 feet square she guessed, with a chair in the center under a rainbow-colored light fixture. She looked at him, and he met her eyes and motioned with his arm toward the chair.

"In here, I travel elsewhere in time. When I take a trip, and make a change to an event, the new timeline moves into place around me. When I return, I remember what was on the timeline before *and* after the correction I made. I retain dual memories, and these are of different density. The old events are like a dream and new happenings after I've changed things are crisp — and part of reality. I guess that's the best I can describe them for someone who hasn't experienced a time trip."

Carrie walked to the chair and touched it. It was a simple, carved wood chair. Ordinary, though of good quality. She looked up at the light fixture, then down to the old metal file cabinets along the back wall. A video monitor on top of a cabinet was streaming live video of Mr. Braggin's house. There were feeds from cameras showing the front door, patio sliding door, a kitchen, and his office.

She scanned the room and saw a printer-copier and office supplies on top of two file cabinets. On one side of the room, a long low shelf was mounted on the wall, within reach of the chair. The wooden shelf was scratched. *No, it's more than scratches*, she thought. It looked as if lines had been roughly carved into it. Beside each line was a jumble of small figurines and trinkets. She saw a tiny pinecone, stones, miniature wooden figures, and a host of oddly-shaped objects.

Carrie looked back at Mr. Braggin. He said nothing, only turned and walked out of the odd room. Carrie glanced around the simple room one more time, then followed Mr. Braggin back into his office. He pushed the wall panel closed and motioned for Carrie to sit again before taking his own seat behind the desk.

"How do you get back?" Carrie asked, the reporter in her kicking into interview mode. "Do you reappear in that chair?"

"No. I wake up upstairs in my bedroom. And coming back is the easiest part of it. Basically, I'm connected to my own time. Everyone is."

"Have other people been in that time-machine room? Or do you travel--"

Peter interrupted, "Others have traveled with me. And, I have allowed a very few people, over my many years, to stay in my time travel room so that they may remember the changes I've made. They awake at home, the day after I took my trip, and they have two sets of memories as I do. Usually they're at my door early in the morning, sometimes confused, but aware of what I've adjusted."

He smiled. "With most people, though, I send them home before I take my trip. Whatever they know at the end of that day is gone from their memories when they awake the next morning. Most of those folks, I never see again. Depending on the correction I've made, and how they found me, many of them don't remember me at all. It's better for me that they don't."

Carrie asked. "How do you know for sure that you've fixed someone's problem if they don't remember you or come back to see you?"

He raised his arm and pointed at a computer perched on the end of his desk. "Gotta love Google," he said. "I know what's changed, but I make a point of confirming what I know through news, employer or resume sites, and social media posts. I double-check to make sure I... well, that I know what I know, and that nothing bizarre has jumped up on the corrected timeline."

Carrie considered his answers, reviewing the few notes she'd taken. *This is crazy, impossible, even*; but she just knew it was the truth.

Mr. Braggin was watching her intently again. "I told you that I help people, and I do. I choose to undertake these little adjustments that impact individual's lives in a big way, even though they hardly affect the bigger world. I don't try to kill baby Hitler or visit a certain grassy knoll in Texas. I just try to do some good for others."

Carrie's heart fluttered, filling with hope. "Who do you help?" she asked, trying not to sound too eager.

"I usually agree to take a trip for people who want to help a friend or change a terrible thing that's happened with family. You know, people are worried about their loved ones, or they regret something, and I want to do what I can."

Carrie knew exactly what he meant about regret. He looked at her intently, his eyes sad, and she flushed. It was as if he was looking *into* her, not *at* her.

"We can talk more about this another time. It seems to me that you're interested in learning more, and I'm happy to talk about time travel, and share my stories about time traveling. Whatever I tell you, like the *time machine*," he used air quotes again, "cannot be published, nor talked about with anyone else."

She saw him frown, and he added, "If the world were to find out what I can do, I'll either be locked up and used by a government agency, or I'd have people lined up around the block. I can't help anyone if the wide-world finds out what I'm able to do."

Carrie nodded, "I understand." Hope rose at his invitation for her to visit again, to *talk another time*.

But, she couldn't wait to ask about Mig, not another second, and seized the moment. "Absolutely, I'll keep what you've told me between us, Mr. Braggin. But, please, help me." Carrie leaned forward, her eyes imploring him. "Please go back and save my husband. Keep Mig from dying. *Please*."

She'd put it all out there. Mr. Braggin didn't look surprised; but, his eyes dropped to his shoes, filling her with foreboding. Carrie waited; her whole body tensed.

After a moment, he said. "I knew that you would ask. We must have *this* conversation, as hard on you as it might be, and which leads me to the next thing that I must share with you. Mrs. Weathers, I'm sorry, but I can't help you in that way. As I said, there are other considerations beyond the rules." He looked up and met her gaze.

Her heart thumped in her chest, quickening as her anxiety rose. A floating sensation engulfed her, and she drew several deep breaths, attempting to ground herself as she exhaled slowly. Her ears rang at high volume.

"Yes. Yes, you can. I know you can," she pleaded. "I believe you. You've just *told me* that you have the ability to do it."

She stood and leaned across the desk toward him. "You said you can go back in time. You admitted it. You *explained* it. So, you *can* bring Mig back!" Her voice came out louder than she'd meant for it to be. Tears rolled freely down her cheeks.

Mr. Braggin stood and slowly made his way around the desk until he was standing in front of her. His now-stern eyes betraying a spark of compassion. "Mrs. Weathers, I know you're disappointed." He reached out his hand and gripped her shoulder. "I'm not trying to be cruel; I assure you. I'm keeping a promise."

"Keeping a promise? To whom?" she asked. Confused, she wiped angrily at her cheeks.

He released her shoulder and took a step away from her. "To Mr. Weathers."

5 – The Promise

Carrie cringed away from Mr. Braggin. *When could he have promised Mig?* When they'd met at the expo, she and Mig had only interviewed the time traveler for thirty minutes. "What do you mean? When did you talk to Mig?" The ringing noise continued, and the light hurt her eyes.

Mr. Braggin sighed, turned away from ger, and looked out the window at nothing. "Your husband came to see me a couple of years after that expo. You had died, and he asked me to take a trip back to save you."

A chill passed through her. A buzzing in her head replaced the ringing. Her stomach lurched, and she feared she would throw up. She sat down quickly, almost missing the chair, leaning slightly to stop herself from falling to the floor.

He continued, "Your husband made me promise that if I brought you back to him, if something happened to him later, I would not change time again. He feared you might be endangered by some kind of twisted karma."

Carrie felt her stomach tighten, grabbed the trash can next to the desk, and vomited violently into it.

The time traveler continued unfazed after handing Carrie a tissue. "You'd been gone a few months, and he wanted you two to be together. You're here because he and I corrected your accident. Unfortunately, in short order he was gone."

Carrie wiped at her mouth, head still hanging over the trash can. She opened her mouth to speak, but clamped it shut as her stomach tightened again.

"He didn't want you to be gone, Mrs. Weathers, even if it meant that in the revised future he might die. Although his death was unrelated, and may have happened without my actions," he shrugged, "I believe my promise to him stands."

Carrie stood and grasped the edge of the desk, her legs like jelly. "I need a moment," she said.

He helped her upright, then led her through the office door and down the hall to a bathroom.

Carrie spent the next ten minutes cleaning up, sobbing, and cleaning up again. When she finally steadied, she walked back into his office, taking her seat on the velvet-cushioned chair. She noticed the trash can was empty and shiny. "I'm okay now," she lied.

He sighed. "I am truly sorry. I thought that you needed to know, to fully understand."

She tried to think of something to change his mind, but nothing came to her. She was angry, but she had no idea at whom she was angry.

"If you're feeling up to it, I need to show you something from your husband." He re-opened the wall panel, and walked into the time travel room.

Slowly, Carrie joined him.

He reached into the top drawer of his file cabinet, which contained manila folders. Withdrawing a folder, he pulled a paper from it and handed the paper to Carrie.

It was a letter from Mig. She recognized his handwriting right away. Mig was left-handed, and Carrie could see the little smears on the paper where his hand had moved across the ink. She ran her finger over the words, her anger dissipating as she touched where Mig's hand had touched.

The letter looked like it had been written quickly, but was legible, and her heart panged as she started reading, recognizing that he had written it, perhaps at Mr. Braggin's prompting, for her to see.

Carrie:

If you're reading this letter, then Peter Braggin has saved your life. I'm so glad you're alive!

If I'm not with you, for whatever reason, I'm sorry.

But, I don't want you going round-and-round with time travel trying to bring me back. I want you to be safe and well.

I know it's hard. I hated life without you, so I know what you're feeling. But please live your life!

God willing, we will see each other again, someday when we're both on the other side.

IDLY,

Mig

She twisted her wedding ring absentmindedly. Their shared way of saying "I do love you" in text messages, IDLY, was engraved inside her wedding ring — both their wedding rings.

"Your husband missed you," he said quietly. "You were in a car accident, died instantly, nothing anyone could do. Mig asked me to go back to that day and ensure he kept you home. It should be apparent to you that I... he succeeded."

Mr. Braggin took the original letter back from Carrie, handing her another paper, which she saw was a copy of Mig's letter. "Take this copy and walk back into my office, please." he said gently.

Mr. Braggin stayed in the time travel room with the original letter and Carrie turned and walked toward his office. The instant her body passed the panel's threshold, sparkling bursts of black — not light, but its opposite — covered the paper, dispersed, and she saw that her hand was empty. The paper was gone! A faint but unpleasant scent filled the air. She couldn't place it, but it reminded her of something rotting.

She turned back toward Mr. Braggin. He showed no surprise. He just waved the letter in his hand.

"Don't worry, Mrs. Weathers. Mig's original letter, and another copy, are still here." He put Mig's letter in the folder and returned it to the file cabinet. He closed and locked the cabinet drawer, then walked out of the little room, directing Carrie back to the velvety chair.

She was a bit shaky on her feet, and he helped her to sit before taking his seat behind the desk.

"Since I've kept the original in the time travel room it can still exist, even though your husband wrote it on a date that, well, had been after he and I's change to the timeline."

He saw her confusion and explained again, "Mig wrote you that letter and I went back to correct the timeline. I made a change and you are alive. In the timeline as it is now, Mr. Weathers didn't write a letter. I keep it in that room so it can still exist. Do you understand?"

Carrie felt the pain behind her eyes increasing. Something hurt, but she couldn't think of the word for it.

He became quiet. She could feel him watching her. She clutched for the trash can, fearing she would vomit again, but nothing came up. After a minute, she raised her head and set down the can. Mr. Braggin handed her tissues, and she wiped her mouth as the ache behind her eyes intensified.

Headache. The word finally came to her through the buzzing and the growing pressure. She blinked in the light.

Without a word, Mr. Braggin switched off the overhead light fixture. Only his desk lamp was lit now. Carrie thought, *He's had people get sick like this before.* Unfortunately, the thought didn't bring her any comfort.

"I don't remember dying." Saying it aloud raised goosebumps on her arms, and she shivered violently.

Mr. Braggin offered, "Memories aren't going to be there for you. It's a seamless change for you, though not for me."

She took a deep breath and implored him, "Why is your promise to Mig stronger than my request for help? Why not let me try? It could work out better for him... and certainly better for me. Please." The *please* spread all the way up to her eyes, and he looked away quickly.

"Look," she continued, "Mig died during his cancer treatment. We caught it so late. I just think maybe if you go back a few years, maybe we can catch it early enough. Does that break your rules? It's just — I feel guilty like it's my fault. I should have seen signs he was sick, but I didn't and we didn't catch it. I just want to go back and get him to the doctor a few years earlier."

She stood and put her hands on the desk, beseeching with her eyes. He would not look at her, and her anger returned. "Do you know what they say about people who lose their spouse, Mr. Braggin? They say that many of them die within six months of each other. *It's been six months.* Six hard months and I can't stand it! I feel like the grief is killing me. I could die if you do nothing."

She fought back tears. Her head ached, and her gut gurgled. She heard him say something under his breath.

"What?" she asked.

"*Déjà vu,*" he said. "Never mind. I'll just say that you and your husband are a lot alike." He corrected himself, "*were* a lot alike."

He watched Carrie intently for a long time, then shook his head. "Mrs. Weathers, I..." He paused and began again, "May I call you *Carrie*?"

She nodded.

"All right, Carrie. Please, you must call me Peter."

The idea of calling him by his first name made her uncomfortable. *It'll be like calling my doctor by his first name*, she thought. She nodded anyway.

"You have family going through this with you. You're not alone, and if you just let time pass--"

"I don't want to," she said firmly. She knew that she sounded like a petulant child and didn't care.

He picked up his coffee mug, looked into it, and set it down hard without taking a drink. The sharp sound startled Carrie. "Why do you want to go against what Mig wanted?"

Carrie cringed as if he'd slapped her. She didn't answer. Tears ran freely, and she didn't wipe them away. Her heart panged in her chest. It had taken her days to screw up the courage to come and see him. She had never been sure she was doing the right thing, and the implication she was going against Mig's wishes hurt too much.

"I think I'd better go," she said softly. "Thank you for your time."

Mr. Braggin walked Carrie to her car in silence.

6 – Upended

After leaving Mr. Braggin's house, Carrie drove around, paying no attention to where she was going. Approaching a little park, she slapped her signal on, and turned into the parking lot. Parking on the far side, she switched off the car. Her emotions whirled and the nausea returned. Closing her eyes, she willed herself not to vomit again.

Her heart ached at the implication that she was going against Mig's wishes, and her anger at Mr. Braggin burned hot. The thought that she had been dead reared its head, filling her with terror. Although Mr. Braggin had explained that she had not ever died in the timeline on which they now lived, she couldn't shake the idea that she had been dead. She opened the door, leaned out and her already-emptied stomach lurched.

When it stopped, she spit several times and closed the door, not caring if anyone had seen. She wiped her mouth and leaned back against the seat. The violent action of her body had disrupted the swirl in her head.

As focus returned, an image of Mig mourning appeared and broke her heart. She didn't like to think of him in pain, any more than she liked feeling grief herself.

She thought of the children and her time with Mig raising the kids; then, of the grandchildren — actually step-grandchildren, although she never thought of them that way. They had made a life together, spending time with the kids, hosting the grandchildren each summer, and living their lives. They'd worked together, gone on adventures together, and loved each other deeply. Every single one of them had mourned her, as they now mourned Mig.

The discovery that her husband had *already done* what she was *trying to do* — that she had died and Mig and Spiky Hair Guy had saved her — horrified her. Knowing that she had been dead and gone, and then wasn't, was dizzying. She searched her memories. She needed to know — or maybe to remind herself — what had happened in her past — or this *new* past — to figure out what felt real.

That doesn't matter, she admonished herself. *What matters is I'm not dead now. Mig doesn't have to be dead now.*

"Please," she said weakly to the empty park. In her mind she imagined Mr. Braggin shaking his head, *no*. Having a solution at hand but knowing that the time traveler was not going to help, was crushing.

Her desperation rose. *I have to convince Mr. Braggin to change Mig's future, his past, our present — whatever it is.*

When Carrie arrived home, she immediately swallowed medicine for her headache, then sat down and — angrily stabbing at the keyboard — drafted the article on Mr. Braggin's time travel ethics. She included quotes that made his work sound theoretical, and omitted anything that might be too revealing. Exposing him to the world wasn't the right thing to do; she would bear the heavy weight of his secret, no matter how frustrated he'd made her. She needed him, and the last thing she was going to do was antagonize him.

Her mind raced along multiple tracks, with trains of thought derailing and crashing as her dead-then-alive situation drifted to mind, raising her anxiety level.

A memory surfaced from her childhood, when she'd almost stepped in front of a car on her way to the bus stop. The close call had made her afraid to cross the road alone. She'd belabored the memory of it for weeks, going over it in her mind with an intense fear that with one more step forward, she would have been hit. She'd even dreamed about dodging cars.

Over time, her revisiting of the near-miss diminished. Eventually, she'd become able to walk to the bus stop again without fear.

She felt anxiety now, like she'd just had a near miss, and her mind was reeling from it. Some part of her knew she should feel relief at being alive, and thankful to Mig, but her mind kept focusing on her death and Mig's death, unsettling her.

Carrie dug deeply into her memories, searching for any trace of dying or of the car accident that had caused it. *Am I supposed to be dead right now?*

She felt a sudden urge to call each of the children and check in on them. She couldn't imagine that they had grieved for her, even buried her, in a different version of this life. Maybe she'd call her brother and sister, too. She'd seen all of them grieving for Mig, and it sickened her to think that they had gone through a similar hard time over her.

I died, then come back, and never felt abnormal...? Mr. Braggin said changes were nearly seamless. Still, Carrie searched her memories for any remnants, finding none.

She thought of Mig, trying to imagine him convincing the time traveler to bring her back. The time traveler had agreed to help him, and here she was. Then, she thought of Mig's letter, and how it had vanished from her hand. She tried to wrap her head around it all.

The time traveler's refusal to help her didn't feel fair. Having the possibility of reversing Mig's death so close made her heart beat faster. Knowing that her life — their lives — had been changed once, she became determined. She *needed* to do for Mig what he had done for her. Somehow, she needed to convince Mr. Braggin to ignore the promise that he made to Mig, and save him.

Although her mind was reeling, she called each of the kids. She let them lead the conversation, just listening, to avoid their picking up on her odd mood. They were all doing well, she was glad to hear.

After the last phone call, Carrie went to bed, flipping on the light in the living room as she passed the switch. Since Mig had died, she'd kept at least one light turned on overnight. She couldn't go to bed in a dark house anymore, not alone.

It took her hours to fall asleep. When she finally slept, a nightmare startled her awake.

In the dream, Carrie had been looking up at the sky from a hole in the ground. Dark clouds drifted by. Dirt started to pour in on top of her. It was covering her, getting in her mouth, eyes and nose, and she felt it pressing her down. She reached her hands through the dirt, trying to claw and pull herself up, but more weight pushed her hands back.

Suddenly, a hand reached down and grabbed her by the shoulder. She recognized it as Mig's hand as he began pulling her upward. She felt her body coming free from the dirt. Up, up, she went. She broke the surface into the air, and the sun was so bright she could only see a figure enveloped in light. That's when she had awakened.

Now, facing Mig's pillow, with her heart still racing from the fight against the falling dirt. She sat upright, staring at the empty pillow. She swallowed a few deep breaths and her heart slowed a little.

Mig had been good at interpreting dreams. Any time one of his siblings or his mother had a strange dream, they called Mig. He had a knack for figuring out what their dream might mean.

Carrie didn't need any help to interpret her nightmare. Then, she began to cry.

7 – Time Marches On

When she climbed out of bed at dawn, Carrie's heart ached and grief swallowed her. She slogged into the new day, forcing herself to make coffee, to get dressed. She wondered how — if — she would ever pull herself together, knowing what she knew now. As if the grief hadn't been bad enough!

After two cups of coffee, she sat at her computer, willing herself to work, starting with reading new emails. She read the first several times before giving up. The grief was getting the best of her, her dream of being buried still had her shook. Knowing she wasn't going to be able to overcome it alone, she decided it might be a good day to make an appointment at the horse therapy farm down the road.

She and Mig had taken the children to horse therapy at the farm several times. When the kids were in high school and acting out, working with the therapist and the horses had helped teach them to express their feelings. It had helped the whole family learn to communicate better.

Carrie had sought out the therapist a few months after Mig passed away. The therapy had allowed Carrie to open up about her grief and, although she hadn't been around horses growing up, she found grooming them to be soothing.

Today, she thought, would be a good day to be with the horses. She needed to calm down. Fortunately, when she asked about an appointment, the farm manager said there was an opening late that afternoon.

When Carrie arrived for her appointment, she discovered that the farm manager, Rosa, was dealing with a serious problem. One of the therapy horses had run into a fence while trying to escape a stray dog chasing it. Rosa told Carrie that by the time animal control had arrived to capture the dog, it and the fence had hurt the horse — an Arabian named Baby Girl. Rosa had called in the veterinarian. He was treating the horse's injuries and, though there would be months of salves, bandages, and medication for Rosa to handle, the vet had said that he expected Baby Girl would recover.

Rosa led Carrie into the barn and to the horse's stall. Baby Girl looked pitiful. She had stitches along her side and the vet was applying bandage across her chest and leg. Rosa comforted the horse, and then closed the stall door.

Rosa then told Carrie they'd continue with the therapy session anyway, with Monty, a paint horse occupying the stall next to Baby Girl. The therapy session turned out to be good for Carrie despite the sad news, and Carrie guessed that it may have been a good distraction for Rosa.

When she drove home an hour later, Carrie felt steadier and ready to get to work. She focused on draft articles, polishing them and publishing several on the news site. Grabbing a notebook and pen, she scribbled a few notes for an article on the horse therapy farm and the dog attack, then stopped working, feeling spent.

Carrie hadn't eaten in a while, but she didn't feel hungry anyway. She decided to go to bed, and began preparing for it.

In the days after Mig died, Carrie had inadvertently developed a nighttime routine. It had started with her doing certain little actions — touching her favorite photo of Mig, holding his wedding ring, fluffing his pillow, and more as the list grew, then saying her prayers, and telling Mig *Goodnight* — before settling into the half-empty bed.

Having the structured "steps" to go through had calmed her at her worst. Now months later, she couldn't go to bed without performing every task. When they were done, she'd settle and, eventually, fall asleep.

This night, Carrie stared at the framed photograph for a long time, tracing Mig's salt-and-pepper hair with her finger. His bright, brown eyes stared out of the photo, which she'd taken one year at the beach. The silver in his hair complemented his golden skin, and he was beaming a genuine smile that reached all the way up to his eyes.

Eventually, she set the frame down on the bedside table and tucked in, facing it. More than an hour passed before her eyes closed, and she drifted off to sleep.

The next morning, Carrie sat down to revise her article on Mr. Braggin, making sure not to give away any of his secrets, nor make his theories sound too valid. Double-checking that no evidence of time travel's reality was given away, she called it done. She wasn't sure if she would even publish it, but it made her feel better to think that she had not entirely lied to Mr. Braggin about writing an article, despite his unveiling of her ulterior motive... and her frustration at his refusal.

As they did so often, Carrie's thoughts turned to Mig. She so missed running articles by Mig before posting them to the news site. They had always worked together on what they published: Mig trusting her to put together the articles from their notes and discussions, and Carrie trusting him to read articles and offer suggestions, or say, "It's good to go." Even though readers liked the articles, Carrie felt that they were incomplete without their give-and-take.

Carrie pushed the computer aside and collapsed on the couch. She turned on the television to distract her uneasy mind, streaming an old comedy film. Instead of relaxing her, no matter what she switched to, the movies became background noise to her racing mind.

If she could convince Mr. Braggin to bring him back, then Mig could be sitting right here on the couch next to her. Just the thought of him being with her made her heart ache. All she had to do was change the time traveler's mind. In the blink of an eye, he could bring Mig back, for her, for the kids and grandchildren. The solution was so close, so frustratingly close. *This man, this time traveler, could return my husband to me; except, he won't. He's standing by this promise Mig extracted from him.*

What had Mig thought about all of this? Carrie guessed that Mig probably thought that it was cool to learn about time travel — as she did. She wished he'd written about that in his letter.

His letter had said for her to live her life. Yet, when he'd written that, he'd been standing next to a time traveler inside a secret room. *Maybe I should stick close to Mr. Braggin, learn more about time travel. I think it's what Mig did, and maybe he'd understand if I want to do the same.*

She wrapped herself in a blanket she kept on the couch. It was one that Mig's mother had given him with the logo of his favorite NFL team, the Broncos, all over it. Feeling its warmth, she imagined how it would feel to be in Mig's arms again. At this thought, she relaxed and — unlike most nights — was soon asleep.

On Saturday morning, Carrie busied herself with household chores. In short order, she was wrapping a bandage around her hand. It turned crimson across her palm, and she sighed, frustrated.

She'd been replacing a broken screen door. The task had already been going badly when the screwdriver slipped. Lucky for her she wasn't pressing too hard, and when it jabbed into her palm it had not cut too deeply.

"Idiot," she said aloud to herself. In her mind, she heard Mig saying, "Hey, don't talk about my wife like that." He would always say that to her when she put herself down. Then he would kiss her. She always kissed him back and said, "I know. I won't."

Now, she flexed the injured hand and surveyed the screen door. It was hanging crooked. She had been tightening the bottom hinge's screw when she had her little accident, and she could see blood on the hinge and screen. *Good job*, she thought sarcastically, *next on my to-do list is scrub blood off the screen door.*

Shaking her head, she picked up the villainous screwdriver and finished tightening the final screws. *If Mig could see me now*, she thought. "Yeah," she said, inadvertently speaking out loud, "but if Mig were here I'd be helping him, not doing it alone."

When she grasped what she'd said, guilt washed over her. She said aloud, as if Mig could hear her, "I don't mean that to blame you, Mig. It's not your fault you aren't here. I just meant with you here, I didn't have to worry about doing stuff I wasn't good at all by myself."

Suddenly aware that she was in hearing range of neighboring houses, speaking aloud to herself, Carrie clamped her lips tightly shut and retreated inside.

Her hand was throbbing by evening. She slathered on cannabinoid oil and applied a new bandage. Making dinner with the bandage on her hand, frying fish and vegetables, she managed to serve them without hurting her hand or bleeding onto the food.

While she ate, she thought about Mig going to see Mr. Braggin, just as she had. How Mig had been grieving, just as she was.

Memories of their life together crawled through her mind, and she examined them suspiciously. *What memories are from after my death?* From what Mr. Braggin had told her, her memories would be seamless, as he'd prevented the accident.

Did he say what day it was when he'd traveled back? "You'd been gone a few months," she remembered Mr. Braggin saying. *But when was the accident?* Asking him the next time she visited was the logical thing to do.

On the other hand, she thought, *none of this feels logical.*

Carrie decided that she would ask Mr. Braggin anyway, if only to understand her situation. *Maybe I'll at least remember something from the day Mig kept me home, when Mr. Braggin saved me.*

Carrie left the light on in the living room and prepared for bed. She went through her routine, then stretched out on top of the blanket. As she set her alarm, she saw the date. She'd been so distracted that she hadn't noticed that the coming day would be her birthday. Her heart fell at the thought of facing yet-another-milestone as a widow.

She closed her eyes and tucked her pillow beneath her cheek, imagining Mig on his pillow facing her. Eventually, she fell asleep with the image of his brown eyes blending into her dreams.

In the morning, Carrie awoke early and started brewing the coffee, bare-footed and wrapped in Mig's bathrobe. She readied the coffee mugs — always two of them — then stood at the counter watching the coffee maker brew.

She knew the kids would be calling today to tell her "Happy birthday." Probably, most of her and Mig's families would call. She planned to be as upbeat as possible and, although Mig's absence on this occasion was excruciating, she focused on how she could catch up on what everyone was doing. Still, as with every phone call over the past six months, she knew she would end up crying with each person who called. They were all still crying. Everybody missed him.

When the coffee maker finished, she poured two mugs of coffee. In her mug, she added a spoonful of brown sugar and a healthy dollop of milk. In Mig's coffee mug, even though he wasn't there to drink it anymore, she fixed it the way he liked it — with a little brown sugar and powdered creamer. She'd made the coffee strong as usual; Mig had preferred strong coffee. Carrie used milk to cut it a bit to suit her taste.

The phone rang for the first time just as she sat down on the living room couch. It was the first of the kids calling to say, "Happy Birthday" and catch Carrie up on their latest news. They talked for close to an hour; the phone ringing again as soon as she'd hung up.

By bedtime, Carrie had talked and cried her way through almost a dozen phone calls. She felt drained, but good. She, and everyone else, liked sharing Mig stories despite the tears they drew. Notwithstanding her red-rimmed eyes, sore cheeks, and heavy heart, she felt grateful for every call.

One of the last calls had been Mig's father. He mentioned that he and his daughter, Mig's sister Tina, had spent the day fishing. As Carrie lay in bed trying to fall asleep, memories floated up of chatting with Mig by the water, of fish caught and released, and of the younger kids with twisted lines in need of untangling.

Even though her memories were happy, and she could see them clearly, tears rolled down her cheeks. *Happy or sad, the tears come*, she thought. She cried herself to sleep, then dreamed of ponds and fishing piers.

8 – Lesson Time

Monday morning, Carrie was once more walking up the time traveler's sidewalk toward his front door. That's how she thought of him now, not the *Spiky Hair Guy* she and Mig had met, but the *Time Traveler*. She had no doubts of Mr. Braggin's capabilities.

Carrie hadn't called Mr. Braggin in advance. She had just driven to his house with the hope that he was home. Now she found herself stopping and standing, then walking a little further up the sidewalk before repeating the pattern. Her mind said, *Keep walking*, but it was also saying *Leave*, just a little fainter.

Carrie knew what she wanted went against Mig's wishes. It was hard to know what she should do — or not do — yet here she was, back to see the time traveler. She wanted to know more, while in the back of her mind hoping that somehow she might convince him to bring Mig back.

As she pushed herself forward, she heard a noise. Looking up, she saw that Mr. Braggin had the door open and was already waiting for her.

"Hello, Carrie," he said kindly. "I've been expecting you."

She almost turned and ran, but instead her feet rooted her to the spot. There was no way he could have known that she would show up. She hadn't even known it until a short time ago.

Mr. Braggin waited a moment, then stepped outside, walked to her, wrapped his hand lightly around her elbow, and led her into the house.

Once they were seated in his office and Carrie had coffee in hand, she relaxed. She thought that maybe it was all right that she was here again, especially since Mr. Braggin had expected her. She wondered how many others he had shocked with his precognition — or whatever it was.

"Mr. Braggin," Carrie began. He inclined his head and she restarted. "Peter... I believe what you've told me. I believe I died." She shivered at hearing herself say it out loud. "I'm just trying to understand... the memories I have... or don't have..."

She took a deep drink of coffee, ignoring the slight burn down her throat as she swallowed.

His expression grew serious. "You'll remember the day Mig stayed home with you. That day when you were supposed to drive to the stadium to cover the 5K race, and Mig kept you from going. That's the day that your car accident didn't happen, and you'll only have memories of staying home. I'm the only one who remembers your accident and its aftermath, and for me they are only smoky memories."

Carrie was shocked that he knew all about that day. Mig must have told him about it after her accident. She wondered how long the two men had talked.

What she remembered, was Mig had convinced her to stay home, and they hadn't covered the event as planned. She remembered that day as one when Mig had been especially cheerful and had grilled steak for their lunch. He'd even broken out her favorite movies, and they hadn't done any work that afternoon. She'd had no idea it was anything more than just another fun day hanging out with Mig, clueless about why; at least, until now.

Carrie sighed, pinching the bridge of her nose to stop any tears. No tears came, and she was surprised to find that she wasn't sad, but hurt. *Mig must have known about time travel if he was involved in saving me.* The thought that Mig had kept it from her was too much. "So, Mig knew that you were a time traveler, and... he didn't tell me."

"No, he didn't know after I corrected the timeline. Once you were back, he had no memories of it," Peter answered.

Carrie breathed a sigh of relief, and just like that, the hurt dissipated. He hadn't hidden it from her; he hadn't remembered.

She saw the time traveler looking at her, but she couldn't think of anything more to ask.

Peter said, "After Mig came to me, we talked and devised a plan to stop you from going out that day. Before my trip, I had Mig write the letter, and he went home. I then set the plan in motion. I traveled back, called then-Mig and, lying that I was a psychic, said I'd had a vision that you were in danger that day, and insisted he keep you home until the next morning.

"Keep in mind that when I traveled back and called then-Mig, he didn't know it was me, or anything about time travel. We'd only met once before that date, at the expo, you recall.

"Carrie, your husband kept you home out of an abundance of caution, and not any foreknowledge of time travel. Likely, if he didn't mention the weird call to you, it may have been because it meant little... just some weirdo calling — which I'm sure you and he experienced many times in your work."

Unsure how to respond, Peter having been the weirdest of them all, Carrie kept quiet. She agreed with Peter's assessment, though, that Mig hadn't mentioned the "psychic" call because he had doubted its truth — yet had liked the idea of spending the day with her.

The time traveler stood, pacing and changing the direction of the conversation as he said, "I know you're here because of my connection to Mig, more than to get to know me." He held up his hand in a stop motion as Carrie's face paled. "It's okay. But you're here and I offer the opportunity to learn more about what I do. I feel I can trust you, just as I came to trust Mig as he and I became acquainted. We spoke quite a bit, him being a curious creature, as are you. If you're interested, I am willing to share what I know."

Carrie nodded. "I'm interested. Where did you start with Mig?"

"At the beginning, I think. I'd like to tell you about my time traveling, starting with my Grandpa. How's that sound?"

"Sure," Carrie answered. Starting at the beginning sounded good to her. Maybe it would make it easier to understand.

"My grandfather was a good man. I try to be a good man. I've mentioned a few of my rules to you, that keep my actions ethical."

Carrie nodded, "I remember."

He continued, "Well, my grandfather didn't so much have rules as advice that he gave me over the years. He thought it was important to help others, and to keep his intentions good. By listening to people, he had a way of discerning if their intentions were also good.

"Grampa discouraged me from traveling for my own desires or gains. It was important to him, and is important to me, to use this gift — and we believe it to be a gift — for positive reasons only. I'm no angel, but I try." Mr. Braggin shrugged. He stopped pacing and sat behind the desk, taking a few deep drinks of his coffee.

Carrie waited and mirrored him, drinking from her mug.

He set down his coffee with an *Ah*, and then spoke in a professorial tone. "This didn't start with me. It started with my grandfather. Grampa and I were close as far back as I can remember. He was a time traveler and picked me to follow in his footsteps. He designed the time-travel room and taught me about its workings. I traveled with him and learned a lot.

"Wait. I want to show you," Peter said, and he jumped up from his seat and disappeared through the office door. In less than a minute, he was back and set a framed photograph on the desk facing her. "That's Grampa and me," he said proudly.

Carrie picked up the photo and stared at it. She turned it at several angles, confused. "That's you and your *grandfather*?" She didn't understand. She recognized Peter, but both men in the photo looked near in age, not more than a decade apart.

Peter smiled. "Yes. Almost like brothers, right?" he asked as he took his seat.

"Yes," Carrie answered.

"Well," he chuckled, "I'm not sure if I mentioned it before, but I'm older than I look. So was Grampa. When he left, he was over a hundred years old, and still could have passed for a *whippersnapper*, as he used to call me." Peter looked at Carrie, but she made no comment.

"Grampa's been gone ten years, by calendar." Then, he added, "I'm in my eighties now, technically."

He's in his eighties? Carrie opened her mouth as if to say something, then closed it without saying a word.

"Yes, I know," he said in response to her silence. He took a sip from his mug. "I don't age like I used to. My aging slowed when I began time travelling in my late teens." He looked into her eyes, a hard look. "Sometimes I feel like that mouse from *Green Mile*. Have you seen that movie?"

She started to nod but stopped, horrified, as the thought of that ancient mouse came to mind. She shuddered. The thought that Peter Braggin was decades older than she, yet looked barely her age, and might live far longer, frightened her.

He continued, "That's not my point, though. I want to tell you about my Grampa because he's the one who was a time traveler and chose me to learn from him and carry on his *corrections*, as he referred to them. As I do, too."

Carrie looked at the photo again. As she turned it in her hands, she noticed the back was inscribed and flipped it over to read it. In a rough scrawl was written,

P.H. - Remember our time together. Love, Grampa.

"P.H.?" she asked.

He explained, "Peter *Horacio*. My middle name is from my Grampa, Alfonso Horacio."

Carrie set down the photo. Peter pulled it close to him, as if protecting it. "Early on, when Grampa was still teaching me how it all worked, he would let me sit in and listen to the people who came to talk with him." Peter gestured around him, "That was right inside this house, in his office that's now my office. They had something they needed to say, and Grampa would listen. If he decided to help them, he'd often let me come along."

Peter explained that his grandfather had stayed under the radar by working as a psychiatrist. "Grampa's patients didn't know that some of their problems were being resolved through time travel. As their psychiatrist, he could ask all types of questions, even ask them to bring a family member in for a session and gather all the life details that he needed to know. Then, he carefully chose who he helped with his special abilities."

Peter furrowed his brow and Carrie wondered what he was thinking. As if responding to her thought, he said, "Grampa did have a problem with his clients going away when he fixed their lives. I'm not talking about clients stopping therapy because their problems went away. I mean people whom Grampa kept from being broken in the first place. They had never come to therapy at all."

Peter laughed, "So, it would affect Grampa's bank account. Because these clients had never come to therapy on the corrected timeline, they had never paid him."

He laughed again. "Grampa would come back from a trip and — always — the next day he would go to the bank and check his account balance. Over time, he had learned to keep gold and silver in the house, to spend frugally, pay with cash, and to keep his bank account as high as possible before a trip. He didn't want to come back to a repossessed house or something."

Carrie shook her head. It seemed unbelievable, the idea of a broke time traveler. She asked, "Why didn't he use what he knew to make more money, and fix it so that he didn't have money problems?"

Peter leaned toward her. He whispered, "Actually, he did a little retroactive investing along the way."

That made them both laugh.

9 – Milestones and Matches

"Okay," Peter said, tapping his hand on the desk edge. He picked up a pen and legal pad, and intently scribbled on it for a moment.

"One of the things that I do when a person comes to see me is I asked them questions about their lives. I did this with Mig, too. I showed him an example timeline, to put what I do in context. I'd like to do the same with you, if you're all right with that, Carrie. I'll ask you questions, then place milestones, reference points, representing your life, on a line. It should help you understand."

Carrie sipped at her coffee, alternating between glancing at Peter and the liquid in her mug, in her mind imagining Mig sitting at the desk, in this weatherworn velvet chair. Except, Peter helped Mig. She pushed this thought down, focusing hard on Peter. "Yes, I can answer."

Peter continued. "All right then."

He drew on a sheet of notebook paper and passed it across the desk. On it were two sketches: one a straight line; the second a line with tree-like branches jutting up from it.

"I see life as a timeline. It is a straight line from when we're born to when it ends. The things that happen are the things that happen, and they become a part of us."

He pointed to the bottom, branching line. "This is how choices are often depicted, as forks in the road, visually speaking, where a person's choices are made. For example, here where the line goes up," he traced a branch with his finger.

"This is where a *choice* is made and a person's life now includes that option only.

"I don't see choices. I see the life as a single line with all events placed upon it. It is what it is." He traced the top line straight across the paper with his finger. "I actually see it, and can see my corrections replace parts of this single, straight, timeline. Replaced parts are gone forever. Didn't happen.

"Carrie, to build the example for you, I'm going to ask you questions and draw a rough version of your timeline. If there's anything you don't want to share, feel free to skip any of my questions." He looked at her cautiously.

"Understood," she said. She took a deep breath, and exhaled slowly. Her gaze was on her mug, but she indicated that she was ready.

"First off, let's talk about significant dates in your life — and Mig's. Tell me what year your first child was born."

"In 1981. Mig's daughter, my stepdaughter, was born. She was already grown when we met. My oldest born, Juli, is four years younger, 1985."

"All right," he said, writing on the pad. "What year was your youngest born?"

"Grace was born in 2000. She was very young when Mig and I married. Mig is... was... her stepfather, but he treated Grace — and her older brother, Dylan, 1996 — like his own."

Peter scribbled again. "How are they holding up?"

"They miss their Dad. They have work and school to keep them busy." Carrie's eyes brimmed with tears. "I know each of them have tough days, too." She almost added, "They're going to get married, have kids, and all kinds of milestones without their Dad here for them," but bit her tongue. Beating up on the time traveler wasn't going to do anything but push him away, and she wanted him to continue explaining.

Peter quizzed Carrie about dates, places, and life events. Each time she responded, she watched as Peter made notations along his drawing of a straight line.

Thinking of good times and family moments, she settled in, answering his questions, and the time passed easily. Then she heard Peter breathe deeply before asking, "Can you tell me about a happy memory? A really good one."

She sipped noisily at the coffee cup. After a moment of letting memories drift through her mind, she settled on one of her favorites. Her voice catching in her throat, she shared it. "When Mig and I were married we had a small ceremony, with just the kids and a few family members. We kept it simple.

"When the minister told Mig to kiss the bride, Mig gave me this soft, perfect kiss that I can still feel on my lips when I think about it." She smiled, although her eyes stung, and tears threatened.

"That's a wonderful memory," Peter said, scribbling on the paper in front of him. "I know it makes you sad, but I think it highlights the love you two shared."

Shared, past tense, she thought. She pushed the pain down as it arrived, which she knew was only saving it for later when she was alone. That, she didn't look forward to experiencing.

He set his pen on the desk and picked up his mug. Taking a drink, and finding it empty, he stood. "I'll fill up our drinks again and give you a minute, then we'll look at your timeline." He took Carrie's mug from her hands as he walked out of the office.

Outside the door, he turned. "Carrie, a grieving person needs to allow themselves to remember the good times as part of healing. Remember that." He didn't wait for a response, which she didn't have anyway.

She heard him walk upstairs to the kitchen and, despite his positive words, alone in the room she began to cry. Floods of agony poured from her.

After a long time, and after her sobs had all but ceased, she wiped her face. Seconds later, she heard Peter coming down the stairs. She forced a smile as Peter returned to his desk and handed across her refilled mug, Carrie's eyes were dry, though tell-tale red and puffy. Having released her anguish, she focused again on Peter's voice.

Pushing the page toward Carrie, Peter showed her that he'd drawn small dots along the straight line, each annotated with the life events she'd mentioned.

"I asked you about dates, places, births, events," he said, tapping the page. These I see as you've lived, straight on, forward every day, since birth."

"What happened to the accident? Can you, please, explain that?"

"Here's *when* I made the correction." He tapped the paper where he had marked the day Mig kept her home, rather than covering the 5K race, "The accident is not part of your timeline, and you two spent this day at home. Simple and logical. One very small change not affecting the previous portion of your long timeline." He slid his finger along the milestones marking the kids' births, their marriage, and other life events.

Carrie stared at the paper, her fingers gripping and releasing the mug in front of her.

"I'll give you another example that might be less stressful for you, hypothetical, all right? Let's say that I were to travel back in time to, say, your wedding day, in the early evening after the ceremony." He tapped the wedding date labeled on the timeline, glancing at her before continuing. "If I were there on your wedding day, and I said something to one of you, or did something like... gave you a flat tire, or changed what happened somehow, I would be replacing one small piece of your timeline. The old would fade away like smoke, and the correction would fall into place."

Carrie stared at the paper, her brow furrowed.

"Let me show it to you a different way," he said, opening a desk drawer. He pulled out a box. Carrie saw that it contained kitchen matches. She watched as he dumped a pile of multicolored matches on his desk and pushed them around. She heard him mutter, "I don't like the red but there's more of them." He continued moving them around, then looked up.

"OK," he started, "This straight line of red-headed matches across my desk represents your life. The match heads are your milestones."

He picked up a match which she saw was blue-topped. "This one represents a piece of timeline that I change, replacing what's there." He carefully balanced the blue match on top of a red one, with the blue match's head on top of the red match head, then pushed the blue match down. It forced the red match to the side, leaving the blue one in line where the red had been.

Peter picked up the red-headed match he'd just displaced and struck it on the box. It burst into flame. He blew it out and smoke drifted up. "That smoke is what is left of that original part of the timeline, replaced by my correction."

He looked up at her with a *"Do you see?"* expression in his eyes.

Carrie's confusion showed on her face.

Peter continued explaining, "Here is another blue match." He picked it up and placed it further up the line of red matches, carefully placing the blue-headed match in place of a red one, then ignited the red-headed match, and blowing it out. "Here is a change rippling up the timeline where another part of your life is changed by the little tweak that I made back here." He pointed at the first blue match. For example, this first blue match is me changing an event, like slashing your tire on your wedding day.

"I wouldn't," he added quickly. "That's just an example. Then, this second blue match is where something else changes later on, like your having to replace the car's tire. It's a minor ripple, in your case not a good thing or a helpful change, but it would be a further timeline correction caused by my previous action. Does this help you understand what I can do? Perhaps also why I am careful to follow my time travel rules?"

Carrie almost felt a light bulb turning on over her head as the concept finally clicked. "Oh!"

He slapped the desk with his hands. "Good. You've got it! Okay, that's a good stopping point. Let's call it a day."

She looked at him, startled. She wanted him to keep talking; the reporter in her wanted more.

"You can come back another day," he added quickly. Carrie relaxed, relieved he was inviting her back again.

"I'll see you again soon. I'm sure you need some time to absorb what I've covered so far."

Carrie set down her coffee, thanked him, and he walked her upstairs and out to her car.

As she backed out of his driveway, she wished she could tell Mig what she'd learned about time travel, and the grief came crashing down.

10 – Time to Think

Early the next morning, Carrie awoke with the urge to go to the beach. She hadn't been anywhere near the ocean since Mig had fallen ill. Answering Peter's questions about their life had triggered a flood of good memories. The beach had been an important place to them, with many happy moments shared there.

She didn't want to see any of the sea and sand without him; but, she felt compelled to go, to be where she, Mig, and the kids had made so many good memories. Maybe it was time to revisit them. In Peter Braggin's voice, she heard, "Remember the good times."

Mig will be with me in spirit, she thought, and that settled it for her. She decided to leave right away, even though it was a Tuesday, too early in the year for the water to be warm, and she had work waiting.

Carrie dressed for the cool weather with jeans and a light jacket. Although it was overcast as she loaded snacks and drinks in the car, the forecast showed sunny skies at the coast, and she chose to wear sandals for easy toe-dipping at the water's edge.

She started driving east toward the ocean. Their favorite place, Topsail Island, was three hours away. There they had enjoyed fishing and swimming with their children and the grandchildren. Her grief grew with every mile, as she recognized spots where they had stopped to eat, or to give the kids a bathroom break, or to buy sunscreen — which they forgot to bring on almost every beach trip. Each memory sent tears streaming down her cheeks.

She made the drive straight through, and by mid-morning she was standing under the pier bawling, and trying to avoid the few people scattered along the beach. With peak tourist season months away, she had a section mostly to herself.

The sky was overcast, so she felt there was little danger of sunburn. She'd forgotten sunscreen, anyway.

She walked up and down the strand, the sky stretching forever. Occasionally, she kicked at a shell with her sandals, her feet warmed by the sun-heated sand. Carrie closed her eyes and could almost feel Mig walking beside her. That made her smile.

She opened her eyes and saw the pier off in the distance. She and Mig had fished on that pier many times over the years.

She thought about a time when they had fished all night while their family slept in their nearby motel room. To avoid waking everyone when they returned from the pier in the early morning hours, she and Mig napped in the car from dawn to breakfast time.

It had been a wonderful night together. What a good time they'd had laughing and talking, fishing, sharing a few beers, taking photos despite the bad lighting, and just enjoying every moment. Even their tiredness and the struggle to sleep in the car's less-than-comfortable seats had been a part of the fun.

Her thoughts turned back to Mig's selflessness working with the time traveler to bring her back.

She was humbled thinking how Mig missed her, and how he had sought out Peter Braggin — just as she had. It made her heart ache.

What now? Mig sent Peter back in time for me. Wouldn't he understand how alike we are, and that I would want to do the same for him?

Those thoughts brought her back to Mig's letter. Of course, he knew she would do the same if something went wrong. He had known that she might end up at Peter Braggin's door.

Thinking of the promise her husband had asked of Peter, she tried to justify doing what *she* wanted, instead of what Mig had wanted. In the letter, Mig had included, "God willing." In Carrie's mind, that phrase meant that Mig had considered his choice to use time travel on a spiritual level. She also knew that he was a man who thought through his actions carefully, and that he would never do something he thought was damning. Yet, his promise showed the opposite: that he feared damning her. *Not so different from the conflict I've been feeling.*

As she strode along the beach, she stopped a few times to pick up shells and look them over before dropping them into the waving, icy water. She kept none. Keeping shells was for holding on to memories. They had many shells at home, brought back from vacations and day trips. Alone on this trip, Carrie didn't want to keep a memory.

She breathed in deeply, the salty air soothing her. Memories stirred, not just of this beach, but of an anniversary trip the two of them had taken to a Virginia beach. There, the air had smelled of fast food and trash, not salty and invigorating like here at Topsail. She and Mig had talked about the smell. It was one of the reasons they had never taken the family to Virginia, instead bringing them repeatedly to the soft sands of Topsail Island. She breathed in deeply again, and savored the fresh scents — and the memories.

She walked back-and-forth for hours. As the sun set, she decided it was time to go, and saw she was far from the beach access spot where she'd parked the car. With the sun went the warmth, and she hugged her jacket tightly around her as she made her way back.

By the time Carrie was seated in her car, she knew that she needed to come to a decision. As much as it pained her, she would not go against what Mig had wanted. She had trusted him in life, and would trust him now. He was the one with strong faith. He'd asked that time travel not be used to save him, long before she'd seen his letter.

Driving home, though, she couldn't help but re-visit the decision, missing his company. Each time, she came to the same conclusion: follow Mig's wishes.

When she pulled into her driveway, it was late. She carried in the few things she'd taken with her to the beach. As soon as she was inside, she kicked off her shoes. Changing into a pair of Mig's pajama bottoms and a baggy T-shirt, Carrie went through her nightly routine before climbing into bed.

As she drifted off, the itchy pillow told her, too late, that she had brought sand into the bed. Chuckling at the mistake, she made a mental note to wash the bedding in the morning.

She said, "Goodnight," to Mig's spot on the bed, and a moment later was sound asleep.

Carrie awoke, unable to focus, heart beating like a hammer.

She'd been in the midst of a vivid dream. Mig had been walking toward her. He looked like himself, wearing clothes she'd seen him wear a dozen times. In the dream, she knew that he was dead in real life.

He approached, smiling and happy to see her, and raised his arms for a hug. When she'd reached out to embrace him, her own joy had jolted her awake.

She sat up, the joy faded and a stinging sadness replaced it. She wept, feeling cheated by awaking before she and Mig could hold each other once more.

She wanted to go back into the dream and tried, but could not, fall back to sleep. After many minutes, she gave up and climbed out of bed. She sobbed as she walked to the kitchen and poured a mug of cold coffee. It was too early to make a pot, the sun hours from rising.

Whatever calm she'd gained from the beach time had dissipated. *Grief is a bear.*

11 – Story Time

The following Friday, Carrie made the drive to Peter Braggin's house. This time, she had called and scheduled to meet. She had heard his smile through the phone as he said he was glad she was returning, and that he looked forward to talking with her more about time travel. From what he'd shared so far, she guessed that he had few people with whom he could speak freely.

She'd arranged the day so that she could go for a horse therapy session early to give her mind a chance to relax and start the day calm. She'd been glad to see that Baby Girl was doing a little better.

As she parked on his driveway and locked her car, she saw Peter standing at the side of the house. He motioned for her to come with him and led her down stone steps onto a patio in his back yard. She recognized it as the patio she'd seen from his office.

Peter sat at a small outdoor table under a blossoming pomegranate tree. The patio was bathed in sunlight, with a garden off to one side and a canopy of trees offering privacy from every direction. She could smell lilac and fruit. The weather had been warm lately, and many plants were blooming early. She tapped her feet on the slate under the table. The stones' colors matched those of the house's stones. All of it looked old, except for the sliding door that she knew led into his office.

Peter had iced tea set out for them. She took a seat across from him and, taking a sip of the tea, was glad to find that it was slightly sweet.

They made small talk. Carrie mentioned that she'd just come from the horse farm. She recounted to Peter how Baby Girl had been injured, yet was recovering. She saw his puzzled expression, and explained about the horse therapy. He asked her about the farm. *Trying to be kind*, she thought.

He asked several questions about the horse and dog, when it had happened, and how the therapist was doing. Carrie answered his questions, filling in details for him. *This is the most we've talked about any subject other than grief or time travel.*

As she was thinking it, Peter switched the conversation to that topic. "There are a few time travel stories I'd like to tell you today," he paused. "If that's okay with you."

"Yes, Mr. — Peter," Carrie said, nodding.

He nodded back. "All right. I think you get the gist of what I do. I'll tell you about a few of the people I've helped. It seems like a logical next thing." He looked up at her and added, "And, selfishly, it gives me an opportunity to talk about my work out loud."

Carrie nodded but said nothing.

"One of the first trips, when I understood enough, was when I was about fifteen years old," Peter said. "Grampa took me back to a year that was before I'd been born. He was helping an old man who had never gone home to his wife after the war."

Carrie wondered which war he meant. Since he was much older than he looked, he must have lived through the times of many more wars than she had.

"This was in the second World War," Peter continued, answering Carrie's un-asked question. "Quite a long time ago.

"Years later, the old man found out his wife had borne him a son, and he was crushed that he'd never had the chance to raise his son with her. He'd come to see Grampa, and Grampa decided to help him. Grampa made a plan to go back to tell the young version of that man about his son, on the day his son was born. Crazy, right?"

Carrie nodded, though she didn't think *crazy* was a strong enough word.

He echoed her nod and continued, "Well, after Grampa and I stopped at the train station to tell this guy — just coming back from the war — that he needed to go home as his wife had just given birth to his son, Grampa took me back a few years further — to 1938 — to the hospital where I'd be born. We didn't do anything there, and I didn't see myself being born or anything like that. But, we just went there.

"The hospital looked brand new. In our time, with years of additions to the building, it was different enough to help me grasp the change. I think that Grampa knew I needed to see something familiar to understand the magnitude of what he was doing, what he was asking me to do.

"I learned a lot that trip, because when we got back, Grampa told me that this guy — the returning soldier whom we'd gone back for — hadn't gone home to raise his son anyway.

"This old man had asked my Grampa to help him be in his kid's life, and then the man had thrown that chance away. He'd never gotten to know his kid after all. Sad." He shook his head. In his eyes, Carrie thought she saw anger.

"Is that rare?" she asked, her voice quiet and catching in her throat. "Do many people squander their second chance?"

He responded, "Most don't. When people fail, though, let me tell you that it takes a toll on me. It always took a toll on Grampa, too. It's frustrating and tests your faith in people."

Peter's second story was more positive. Grampa had sent Peter back to help a man named John repair his relationship with his father. They'd fought over a young woman whom John had dated in high school. It was only one date, and John had married someone else and had a few kids, but John's father never got over him dating her.

It had not much to do with the girl, but with the girl's dad, who had fired John's father a few years earlier. John admitted he'd gone out with her only to spite his dad. He knew that the rift between them was his fault and felt that it was his responsibility to fix it.

"So, Grampa, John and I made a plan and I went back to his high-school days and had a talk with younger-John. John didn't take the girl out, he and his father ended up having a good relationship, and John's kids ended up with a grandfather," Peter said.

"That's incredible," Carrie said. "So simple. I mean, I don't mean you time traveling, I mean... A little thing and it made everything better for this John and his family."

"Absolutely right," Peter said. "This next one I'll share is a rough one," he said, sighing, "But I'm going to tell it anyway.

"After Grampa was gone and it was just me, a young man came to see me. He had lost his mother to his abusive father.

"Fixing abuse is always tough, and often impacts other people. Kids end up in foster care, or spouses end up... well, it changes more."

He fell quiet, and she wondered what he wasn't saying. She waited for him to continue and sipped at her tea.

Peter cleared his throat. "So, this young man, Brad, was missing his mother and feeling guilty. He told me his life story, and I was inclined to help him. I went back to his childhood and our plan was for Brad to report the abuse so that he and his mother could escape.

"I went back and talked with the boy," Peter said, "Kids are easier, because I can be honest and tell them that I've traveled through time to help them. The only hard part is not raising the suspicions of the adults around them.

"After I convinced kid-Brad to report his father, I didn't leave the past right away as he and I had agreed. Instead, I followed Brad — the younger him — around. He was a kid, after all, and it was really a tough thing he had to do. Somebody must believe him when he reported the abuse. His mother had to tell the truth to authorities, potentially, and they both needed to get away, escape. I was worried, so I spent extra time keeping an eye on the kid."

He paused. His voice was getting thicker as he spoke. Carrie could see it was a tough story for him to tell. She was eager to hear it, and moved to the edge of her seat.

"Well, Brad — kid Brad — goes to the police. The police went to his mother, and she denied the abuse. Brad kept telling people — his teachers, his grandparents, the police again — and nothing changed. He and his mother were still stuck.

"A couple of weeks passed, and nothing was getting better for this boy. It was frustrating. I talked with him about once a week and encouraged him, and I hoped someone would listen so that he and his mother could be saved, and I could return to my time.

Peter sighed. Looking directly at Carrie, he shrugged his shoulders, "I followed Brad's father to work one day. I waited until he and I were alone at a bus stop, and I pushed him in front of a bus."

Carrie stood up in shock. Her mouth hung open as she looked down at him. Peter only nodded, returning the look. She closed her mouth and, after a few moments, sat down.

"I'm sorry, Peter," was all that she could think to say. Carrie should have been horrified, but wasn't. Her thoughts flickered back to a boy from her neighborhood. She'd grown up down the street from him and his family. She couldn't remember his name, but she remembered that he had been an average boy, until one day his father had beaten him so severely that his mental abilities were affected, and the boy became unable to even attend school after the attack. The boy's parents were never charged, nor the boy removed from the home. Thinking of him, Carrie felt more pity for what Peter must have felt compelled to do than for the man he had murdered.

Peter seemed surprised at her reaction, smiled weakly and said, "Thank you."

He took a drink. Clearing his throat, he added, "I came back a few minutes after that. I couldn't take the chance of getting arrested. It wasn't what I wanted or expected to do, but it did end up helping both Brad and his mother. At least, it helped them *enough*."

His next story had a more positive tone. It was a trip he'd taken earlier than the one for Brad. This trip had to do with a couple Peter had helped on his own while Grampa was off on a trip for someone else.

A middle-aged couple had come to ask for help for a friend. Their friend — a woman named Jenny — had become homeless after paying off her parents' medical bills and final expenses. She had lost everything and was struggling to get back on her feet. The couple asked Peter for a chance to save her from her problems by encouraging Jenny's parents to get life insurance.

Peter told the story lightly, laughing along the way. He called it 'an easy problem' and talked about how in his experience fixing a money problem was a piece of cake, comparatively. He'd gone back to talk with Jenny and her parents about protecting her future. They had one conversation, the parents set up life insurance, and that was all that it took to fix her future problems. "In our time now," Peter said, "Jenny is fine. She was never homeless and has lived an ordinary life."

Carrie's thoughts turned to the costs of Mig's medical care. Maybe there was a money-related loophole she could use to convince Peter to change the timeline so that she and Mig would have had more money for his fight against the cancer. *No, that wouldn't have helped*, she knew. They'd caught the cancer so late. Only catching the disease earlier would have made a difference. *Could make a difference*, she corrected herself.

She knew that there wasn't a loophole for her to argue. Besides, she didn't want to manipulate Peter. *What if he sends me away? Or worse, wipes my memory of all of this?*

She shook her head, trying to clear her mind and get back to the present and Peter's story. Peter was looking at her, and she turned away from him. She felt wetness on her cheeks and wiped it away. "I'm sorry. Please continue," she said.

Without commenting on her tears, Peter went on, "In that instance, I allowed the couple to stay in the time travel room with me, so they remembered what had been, and what became, for them and their friend.

"Later," Peter said, "the couple stopped by to thank me. I again reminded them to keep what they knew to themselves; to never mention it to Jenny, either. There was no sense drawing unwanted attention. As far as I know, they've complied."

He added, "Although government folks show up from time-to-time, none of my clients has ever talked. Still, I keep the number of people in-the-loop to a minimum, just as Grampa did."

Peter jumped up from his chair. In an overly cheery voice he said, "Let's hit the kitchen and get some more tea. Or coffee, if you prefer."

Carrie nodded, rose, and followed him inside and upstairs to his kitchen. In the kitchen, Peter talked about his public lectures. He explained that he had not followed in his grandfather's footsteps in the same cautious way. While his Grampa had chosen a profession that let him stay under the radar, Peter had decided to speak out publicly about time travel and the need for ethical use. He'd become a kind of researcher, sometimes professor, to ensure that if — or when — time travel got out into the world, his papers and presentations would be out there to educate.

Peter pointed down the stairs, "You know, my time travel room is just a room, technologically speaking," Peter explained. "Grampa set it up and used it. I also use it, as I've said. The room is more about being in a controlled, non-distracting environment.

"It isn't that it had any power of its own to begin with, or that it is the only place from which one could time travel. But, by designating it as a time travel room, setting it up, using it, and sharing Grampa's and my own abilities *with it,* in a way, that room has developed a type of boundary over the years. That's why I can keep file cabinets inside it and protect the contents. It's also why there is a boundary when leaving the room and stepping into my office.

"If I stopped using it, the protective energy would eventually fade. Maybe in a hundred years or so, my files would just disappear." He laughed, "Probably the file cabinets with them, now that I think about it." He paused, then added, "The trinkets on my shelf would go away too."

Carrie listened, but she was thinking of the many and varied items on his time travel room shelf, wondering if each had a story.

He continued, "Now those trinkets, they are only there to help me focus. They have no power, per se, but are prompts for me to concentrate, or to let my mind go blank-ish, depending on what I'm planning to do in the past.

"Sometimes I pick up new little bits to add. For example, the other day I picked up a rock that caught my eye. It has a pattern on it that reminds me of a New York skyline. I might use it if I'm traveling to the past in New York, for example, and want to hold it in my hand to give myself a little extra focus, But, the rock is just a rock — a tool I might use."

"You can go other places? Like, not just around here?"

"Yes. I can go anywhere, and come back from anywhere. To travel, I focus on a time and place. To return, there is a connection from where I am to where I belong. But, I don't need the room or the trinkets, technically, and when I come back I don't need to be returning from a specific place... like in movies where they have to stand on the same spot from which they first arrived."

Peter took a break from storytelling to refill his and Carrie's tea glasses, and she found herself again thinking about how she might leverage Peter's stories to convince him to help her. She tried to put together a compelling argument for him to bring back Mig, despite the part of her that knew she should honor Mig's wishes. *It's hard to be with a time traveler and not ask for a correction.*

When Peter returned and handed her the tea glass, she only had half an argument ready and her internal fight still raged. Before she could say a word, though, he cut her off.

"I know you're conflicted about Mig's promise. I appreciate that you're hurting." He looked directly at her, "I saw Mig when he was hurting too. This timeline isn't what he wanted, Carrie. In *no way* did he mean for you to be hurt. Like his letter said, though, he was glad to have you alive, no matter what happened next. He told me that you two trusted each other, so I know you'll trust him now, and please, trust me by not asking me to break my promise."

After a moment, she nodded.

He launched into his next tale. They talked through the afternoon, him telling her about a few more of his travels, and about his grandfather, as she asked questions.

It was getting dark when she left the time traveler's house and drove home.

Peter pushed his half-full dinner plate aside. He scowled at nothing in particular, then pushed his chair back and walked into the living room.

Pacing, he glanced at the framed photograph of his grandfather on a side table by the fireplace. Each time he passed, the older man in the picture seemed to be staring at him. Finally, Peter stopped pacing and picked up the frame. "You know, Grampa," he said aloud, "You'd do the same thing I'm doing. I have to keep my word, regardless how much someone else suffers."

The visage didn't give him an answer; but, Peter knew how to get one. He set the frame down and walked purposefully down the stairs and into his office.

His grandfather, Alfonso Horacio, had years ago gone forward in time, and stayed there. Peter remembered the day that his Grampa had announced that he was sick and, rather than stay and fight what he said would be "a losing battle," he had decided to go forward.

"Maybe I'll find a cure, maybe not. But, you and I will, in that way, have more years together. I'm going forward twenty years, P.H., and you must come and see me after twenty years have gone by."

When Peter protested, the old man said, "You should not have to watch me deteriorate. And, I will see you when you catch up."

The day his Grampa left on his special trip, he put his arm around Peter, and told Peter that he was not to worry. He'd patted Peter on the back, ruffled his hair as if he was still a small boy. "You're a good man, you've listened to my ramblings and used time travel well. I don't doubt you'll be fine without me."

He gave Peter a set of instructions to reach him, through classified ads in the Denver newspaper. As a child, Alfonso had moved from New Mexico to Denver, Colorado, and considered it his *hometown* despite their years in North Carolina. "I will watch for word from you, and come if you need me."

Since his departure, once a year on his Grampa's birthday, Peter placed an ad in the newspaper with a birthday hello: 'Happy Birthday, Love, P.H.' Twice, Peter had placed ads asking for help. Both times, Alfonso had come.

Navigating to the news website, Peter carefully worded a message. It read:

'Happy early birthday, Grampa. Let's talk soon. P.H.'

12 – Opportunity

On Tuesday afternoon, Carrie had just sat down on the couch, lunch plate in hand, when her cell phone rang.

"Hello, Carrie," Peter said when she answered, "May I ask you for a favor?"

Without waiting for a response, Peter immediately launched into his request. She detected shades of Spiky Hair Guy as he spoke. "I met with a young man today, and I'm considering making a correction for him," Peter began. "but I would like you to come and help me with his wife."

"With... his... wife? Um, hang on a second and then I need you to give me the details." Carrie took her plate back to the kitchen and popped it in the microwave. She had a feeling she wouldn't be getting to eat lunch until Peter clarified what this favor regarding somebody's wife would entail. She returned to the couch and said, "Okay, tell me more about this favor."

"A little while ago, I had an appointment with this man, Buddy something, mid-40s, who had called last week and asked if he could see me. Apparently, he'd read about my work online. Well, we got to talking... he and my semi-crazy persona, actually, and Buddy said that he really hoped I could travel through time, because his wife had asked for a divorce and he didn't want to lose her."

"Okay..." Carrie said, since Peter had paused and she believed he wanted acknowledgement that she was listening.

"Well, he said the divorce was all his fault. He explained that last year, he had accepted a new job that paid better. He'd taken the job for the money, and he and his wife Tammy had agreed that it was a good idea. That new job turned out to be a bad move."

"Go on," Carrie said, her stomach rumbling.

"According to Buddy, the job turned out to be fraught with high-end clothing costs, out-of-town trips, and un-reimbursed expenses, among other things. He and Tammy are feeling the strain on their finances, and see each other less than when he had his prior job. Plus, they dug a hole by spending part of his expected salary on home improvements. Buddy told me that last week Tammy said she wasn't happy anymore and she wanted a divorce."

"So she's asked for the divorce," Carrie interjected. "How can I help with that? It's up to her, isn't it? Or, are you thinking that if you change Buddy's job, she might reach a different conclusion? Do you really think the job is the problem? What did you think of Buddy?"

"That's a lot of questions, Carrie. Bear with me and I think I can answer them."

"All right. Go on, Peter."

"Buddy's belief is that if he hadn't left his old job, where he had weekends off and they were getting by financially, she wouldn't have become this unhappy. He has asked me to go back to the day that it was offered to him, and stop him from taking it.

"I spoken with Buddy for a while and I believed he is genuinely eager to save his marriage. What I don't know is his wife's point of view. She may have other issues with Buddy, so that question of yours I can't answer... without you doing me the favor I mentioned."

"Which is?"

"I don't want to change anything until I know more about how his wife feels. When Buddy prepared to leave, I suggested that tonight he should take his wife out to dinner, and he should talk with her about giving their marriage one more try. After that, he can come back and see me, and tell me how it went. Buddy told me that he would, and that his wife loved a little Italian joint in town called Roselli's.

"Then he left, and I called you, and here we are," Peter said, wrapping up his story. "You're an investigative person by nature. Can you meet me and we'll eavesdrop on Buddy and Tammy over dinner?"

Carrie wasn't sure what to say. She stared at the phone and tried to think of a response. On the one hand, it sounded bizarre. On the other hand, it could be an interesting opportunity for her to see Peter in action, doing his whole planning-for-time-traveling thing.

Peter continued before she answered. "I'm going to email you an address," he said, "If you're interested, then I'll see you there at 7 o'clock tonight."

"Okay. Um, I'll be there. Good-bye," Carrie said, and ended the phone call before she could change her mind.

Removing her lunch from the microwave without heating it, she wrapped it and tossed it in the refrigerator. Her stomach flopping nervously, she didn't want food now.

At 7 o'clock that evening, Peter and Carrie were seated in a cozy coffee shop across the street from Roselli's Italian Restaurant. Both had arrived early.

Peter filled Carrie in on his conversation with Buddy in more detail, then reiterated in a low voice, "My biggest concern is that if his wife truly wants a divorce, it would not be in her best interests for me to help Buddy. It's not just about avoiding ripples in this case. It's ensuring I'm not taking away her freedom to make that choice."

Carrie agreed that it was a good call to check out the wife's side of things. Peter told Carrie that he hoped that they would soon see the couple arrive at Roselli's.

"If we can be strategically seated near Buddy and Tammy and listen to their conversation — especially Tammy's side of things — we can sort out what Tammy's wants."

Working in their favor was the privacy-oriented decor of Roselli's, with its half walls, fake plastic plants, and low lighting, Carrie and Peter could avoid being seen. They both knew that if Buddy saw Peter, the plan might fall apart.

They were drinking their second cups of coffee when Peter spotted Buddy and a woman — presumably his wife — walking into Roselli's. "Well, that's a good sign," Peter said. "She agreed to come to dinner with him. Otherwise, our evening would have been wasted... especially yours. I appreciate your coming along. Two heads are better than one."

He stood and drained his coffee mug in a single gulp. Motioning to Carrie, Peter said, "Drink up. Let's go and see what we can find out." He dropped a tip on the table and walked out.

Hurriedly, Carrie stood, drank the rest of her coffee quickly, and followed him. *Even without the Spiky Hair Guy persona he's still socially awkward*, she thought.

Roselli's wasn't busy, and there were no other diners waiting to be seated when Carrie and Peter walked in. The hostess led them to where Peter requested — a table behind the already-ordering couple.

Peter and Carrie sat quietly, eavesdropping on the couple's exchanges. Carrie was glad to hear the man address the woman as Tammy, confirming it was his wife. Otherwise, it could have been an easy answer for Peter to decline to help him.

They listened to Buddy and Tammy's conversation, speaking in low voices when the server came to take their orders. Carrie felt like a mix of reporter and spy.

Carrie was pleased to discover that throughout the dinner the man and his wife got along fine. Aside from a general tension in their conversations, they talked to each other about household things and work. The word "divorce" didn't enter their conversation until dessert, when Tammy commented how nice the dinner had been, and how different things would be for them after the divorce. She sounded sad, too, just as Peter had described Buddy to be.

After Buddy and Tammy left the restaurant, Carrie said, "I think doing what you can to circumvent their divorce would be a good thing. His wife sounded sad about it." She paused, "What do you think, Peter?"

He nodded. "I agree."

Carrie liked the fact that Peter was going to help this couple, and that she could participate. Then, as she pictured Buddy and Tammy regaining their happiness, her heart panged with grief as she remembered how happy she and Mig had been. She stabbed at her plate, piercing a ravioli, willing her mind to clear as she focused on the unfortunate raviolis.

She and Peter finished the meal in silence.

As they walked out of the restaurant, he said, "All right, thank you for helping me sort Tammy out. The next step is for me to do background work and, when I've made a plan for past-Buddy, would you like to help me when I take my trip to correct Buddy and Tammy's situation?"

Carrie answered quickly, "I'm nervous, but I'm in." before she could think about it too long.

"I'm happy to hear it! You go home, and we'll meet tomorrow for the trip. I'll travel, you stay in the time travel room, and you'll remember all this, and more."

As they walked to their cars, Carrie thought about how Peter would change the couple's lives. *What will that be like?* Her curiosity kicked in and she was glad that she'd agreed to take part, despite her anxiety about seeing events change.

Peter was happy that she'd agreed, if his bouncy walk was any indication.

Reaching their cars, he leaned on his car's roof and said, "You know, I haven't had someone working with me in a while," he added quickly, "I mean since Grampa," and climbed into his car.

Carrie thought the way he said the last part sounded off, like he was lying. She wondered who else had helped Peter as she was. *If not his Grampa, who? Was it Mig?* She wasn't sure Peter would tell her, but maybe she'd ask him some other time.

The next day, Carrie received a phone call from Peter that lasted a few seconds. "Can you get to my house by 8:45 tonight?" he asked. She said she would be there and ended the phone call.

Carrie took a deep breath and tried to prepare herself for something for which she had no idea how to prepare.

Arriving at Peter's house a few minutes early, she parked at the top of the driveway. She walked around to the patio, and Peter ushered her inside through the sliding doors. They settled in his office, Carrie in the velvet chair and Peter in his customary seat behind the desk.

She noted how differently Peter was acting compared to when she'd first come to see him — when she still thought of him as Spiky Hair Guy. He displayed confidence and was behaving rationally. She wasn't usually so observant. Mig was the one who had been a good judge of character and could see people for who they really were. She wondered how long it had taken Mig to break through the Spiky Hair Guy persona when he had come to Peter's.

"Buddy should be arriving in about fifteen minutes and I'll be asking him more questions, mostly to confirm what we already know about Tammy. I also need to get the specific time and date of his job interview last year, to make sure I arrive near the right moment for the impact I need to make. I need to convince past-Buddy not to accept the job offer."

"What will I do when you go back?"

"For now, I'd like you to hide in the time travel room and listen to my conversation with Buddy. Then, once he leaves, you'll stay overnight in the time travel room while I travel back."

The doorbell rang, signaling Buddy's arrival. Peter opened the panel and led Carrie into the secret room. He gave Carrie headphones he'd connected to the security system, moving the wooden chair from the center of the room over to where she could sit comfortably. He hit a switch, and instead of four camera streams, she saw the view into his office. "You'll be able to hear he and I speaking. I'll go let him in, and see you soon," he said as he closed the secret panel.

A few minutes later, the video screen showed Peter and Buddy entering the office and sitting down. She heard them clearly through the headset.

She kept as quiet and still as she could, feeling spy-like again.

Carrie learned that Buddy's full name was Theodore Morris. She listened as Peter carefully explained how he planned to repair Buddy's error in switching jobs. After extracting the job interview details, Peter told Buddy that to be most effective, he needed to know what was going on with "back then" Buddy — little things that Peter could use to trigger then-Buddy into declining the job offer.

Peter quizzed Buddy briefly, then wrapped up the conversation by telling Buddy that it had been a pleasure knowing him. "You won't remember anything about us meeting when you wake up tomorrow morning." They shook hands, and Buddy wished Peter good luck before leaving.

After the man left, Carrie came through the secret panel, and Peter turned toward her. "Okay," he said. "He's all set. I think his wife is all set. Time to finalize my plan."

Mr. Braggin reached over and pulled a notebook off the shelf behind his desk. "I need to make sure I have a convincing argument to give this guy and keep him from taking that job. Give me about twenty minutes to finish my preparations. I hope you don't mind a short wait."

Carrie nodded. "Sure. If you don't mind, I'll make a pot of coffee."

"Coffee sounds good," Peter said. "There's sandwich stuff in the refrigerator and bread on the counter if you're hungry."

"Thank you, I'll make sandwiches," Carrie responded, ignoring her anxiety at the delay — which would give her more time to contemplate what was coming. "I don't know, but I'm guessing it's going to be an eventful evening, and we will need the fuel."

He thanked her again for being there, and Carrie headed upstairs to the kitchen. She made sandwiches, took one to Peter's office, and left it on his desk. He didn't even look up.

Returning to the kitchen, she took a seat in one of the tall chairs at the counter. She thought of an idea for an article and jotted a few notes while she ate. Then, her thoughts turned to the previous night's eavesdropping, and poor Tammy. She hoped Peter was making a good plan, and checked the time. The next few minutes passed slowly, with Carrie drinking too much coffee, looking at the clock, and fidgeting in anticipation of the coming time travel adventure.

Then, Carrie heard Peter yell, "I'm ready!" She jumped up with a start, feeling a little wobbly as she stood. Her legs had fallen asleep.

"Be right there," she responded. She took a swig of coffee, then another. Still feeling pins-and-needles, she carefully descended the stairs for her first foray into time travel; at least, the first she would remember. That thought brought her to full alertness, her heart rate increasing.

As Carrie walked into the office, she saw that Peter had the secret panel to the time travel room open. He explained his plan. "I'll be going back to the day Buddy went on his interview for the job he regrets accepting. I plan to run into him as he is leaving the interview and pretend that I work at that company."

"Sounds good so far," Carrie said.

"I think that if I can corner him well enough, or maybe get him to join me for a drink nearby, I plan to complain about how I hate working at that company, how the hours are bad, that

I never see my wife, and the money doesn't go as far because they cheat employees by not reimbursing expenses, how I feel like I make less money than ever--"

"So," Carrie interrupted, "You're basically going to say to the past version of Buddy what the present version of him told you."

"I sure am," Peter laughed. "Experience tells me that will work. He should respond to hearing the kinds of things that he would say."

"I have a suggestion," Carrie said. "Play up the part about never seeing his wife and the rift the job causes between them. Since his fear of losing Tammy is what brought him to you, I'd suggest you make him think of her. Maybe even include the word *divorce* in what you say."

"That's an excellent suggestion," Peter said. He grabbed a chunk of sandwich from the plate on his desk and popped it into his mouth. He chewed quickly and swallowed, then took a gulp of coffee, absentmindedly setting the coffee mug down on the bookshelf behind his desk.

Carrie watched as he picked up a metal, old-looking fan from the floor and place it on his desk. He stooped to plug it in, and it began spinning, emitting a loud burr. "White noise," Peter said. "Because you're staying in the room with me for the first time, I'm adding a little extra background sound on which I can concentrate."

He scooped papers up from his desk, avoiding the wind from the fan, and tossing them into a manila folder. Walking into the time travel room, Peter motioned for Carrie to follow. She walked into the room behind him.

Peter shut the panel, but she could still hear the loud hum of the fan.

Peter opened one of the file cabinet drawers and slid the manila folder into it. He picked up a piece of paper from a stack next to the printer, then fished a pen out of his pocket. "Write a note to yourself about what we're going to do," he instructed, handing the paper and pen to Carrie.

She wrote a brief note, signed it, and handed it to him. He tossed it onto the top of his printer-copier and ran a copy, copied his own note, then tossed them into the file drawer and slid it shut.

"Okay," he said. "Tomorrow you'll see how those work." Thinking, he added, "Again."

"Okay," she said, hugging herself with both arms. Now that the time had come, she couldn't wait for it to be over. Her reporter side was hiding somewhere, and the rest of her felt like a deer in headlights.

Peter said, "Let me go over what's going to happen. You'll be here, inside the time travel room. I'm going to sit down on the chair in the center of the room. I'll fiddle with the small items on his shelf, calm myself, and then I'll disappear.

"Whatever happens, please try not to speak or make noise. I'm going back less than a year, and only about twenty miles as the crow flies, so it will take me just a moment of concentration. Then, I'll go, you'll see a *poof*, much like when the copy of Mig's letter disappeared in your hand."

Then he pointed to the corner of the room. "I need you to stay back by the file cabinet and copier. I've left a pillow and blanket there for you. Staying back is to keep you out of my line-of-sight, so I can concentrate. Just get as comfortable as you can, sleep as soon as you can."

"Um," Carrie said, her brain suddenly blank.

"There's nothing to worry about. You're in no danger of being pulled along with me, or anything like that. It can't happen by accident."

Carrie looked around the small space, heart thumping, and, she was dismayed to find, palms sweating. She thought of Peter puffing out like Mig's note. Suddenly, her fear overcame her. "Wait, I can't do this."

Peter let out a sigh and stared at her. There was no anger or disappointment in his eyes, which she was glad to see. Calmly, he said, "No problem. Believe me, I understand how far-out all of this can feel. There will be other chances, so don't worry about it."

Carrie nodded, backing toward the opening in the wall. "Thank you," she whispered.

"Do you want to take a few minutes, or are you sure you won't stay?"

"I want to go. I'm sorry." Carrie stepped out of the time travel room into the office and started to close the wall panel.

Peter stopped her, grasping the panel edge. He said kindly, "I understand. Stay in the house if you like. Have a drink and go to sleep. If all goes well — and it will — you will wake up in your own bed. If you want to go home, go ahead and please lock my front door. Either way, I'll see you in the morning."

"Okay," Carrie said breathlessly.

Peter shut the panel. Carrie left immediately, locking the front door behind her. She drove home, trying not to think about what was happening with Peter right then.

Despite the late hour, she made a pot of coffee, and sat up thinking.

Just before 1 A.M., she walked into the bedroom, went through her nightly routine, and snuggled down into the blankets. She immediately fell asleep.

K. F. Whatley

13 – Opportunity Lost

When Carrie awoke at 9 o'clock the next morning, she was feeling energetic, more than usual, and sat down to work right away. She didn't have any appointments and was glad to have the day to focus on draft articles and email.

At lunchtime, Peter turned up on Carrie's doorstep with a restaurant bag in his hand. Carrie was surprised to see him but invited him inside.

"Good afternoon," Peter said.

"Good afternoon," Carrie responded, eyeing the bag.

"I was hoping you'd be working at home today," he said, handing the bag to her. "I brought lunch."

"Oh, um, thank you," Carrie said, despite her discomfort that Peter would drop by with food, unannounced.

"So, what did you do yesterday?" he asked cheerily, still standing inside the front door.

"Oh, not much," Carrie responded. "I worked, picked up groceries. Stuff like that."

"Right. Right," he said. Carrie saw him smirking, and wondered what was funny. "How about the day before?"

"Nothing in particular..."

Then, he asked, "So, we didn't meet for dinner at Roselli's the other night?"

Carrie flushed, "What? No! I..." She felt like a light bulb turned on over her head. *He must have made one of his corrections*. Nervously, she asked, "What did you change and what don't I remember?"

"Let's eat first," Peter said, then he turned and walked toward her kitchen. "Is your kitchen this way?" He didn't wait for her answer.

Carrie didn't want to eat first, she wanted to know what was going on. Following him into the kitchen, she grabbed forks and plates while he unpacked two containers of food. It was pasta from Roselli's restaurant.

Peter said, "I thought we should celebrate, Carrie."

She looked at him, puzzled. "Mr. Br... Peter, celebrate what?"

Peter grinned, "Yeah, you don't know. I'll explain what and why we're celebrating. And even why we're eating take-out from Roselli's." He tapped the restaurant logo on the bag.

Crap, thought Carrie. She knew that he must have time traveled, and — worse — there was something she used to know that she didn't know anymore. "I'm not much of a drinker, but I have this sudden urge to add whiskey to my coffee."

"All is well, Carrie," he chuckled. "I took a trip last night. I invited you to stay in the time travel room and watch time change. You weren't ready, though, and the last I saw of you was the nervous look on your face."

Carrie's mouth hung open. Before she could respond, Peter continued. She focused on what he was saying, trying to distract herself from the anxiety rising in her chest. "Yesterday, you helped me change time for a man named Buddy. You listened as I interviewed him and were helpful in planning my correction. That was yesterday.

"The day before yesterday, we went to dinner at Roselli's, you and I--" he stopped as Carrie flushed, and shook his head. "Nothing sordid, young lady. We only went out to dinner so you and I could follow Buddy and his wife Tammy, and eavesdrop on their conversation."

He paused, and Carrie was glad. She needed a minute to absorb what he'd just shared, including the fact that she'd lost two days.

"No memory at all?" Peter asked.

Carrie shook her head. She heard buzzing inside her ears, and tried to calm herself.

"Don't be frightened. You can't remember what, as of today," he looked at his watch absentmindedly, "never happened. That's normal, and I'll happily fill in the blanks."

"I don't remember going to Roselli's, or Buddy and his wife, or any of it," she blurted. Her brow furrowed as she thought hard of the previous two days. "In fact, I remember working and buying groceries yesterday. I even made myself a BLT for dinner last night."

"Good!" Peter exclaimed. "Well, my client's problem is solved, and you're no worse for the wear."

Carrie wasn't sure if that was exactly true. She felt a little worse for the wear, dizzied at knowing she'd done things that she couldn't recall. "Okay, um, so you set everything right for this Buddy." She took a deep breath and released it slowly. "Tell me how you did it."

Peter tried to wave her off, digging into the large portion of pasta in front of him. She insisted and, after sliding a cup of coffee his way, he swallowed hard and said, "All is fine. I promise that you'll be okay with what you've forgotten. Or, well, actually never knew." He grinned again, and Carrie sat down slowly, fork in hand, waiting for him to tell his tale.

Peter explained how Buddy had approached him for help, wanting to avoid what he felt was a pending divorce. Peter had then enlisted Carrie's help to follow Buddy and his wife. She had helped him determine that Buddy's wife wasn't eager for a divorce, and then Peter had traveled to help Buddy. "You changed your mind about staying in the time travel room while I left, which is why you don't remember.

"I put forth a pretty good argument and convinced last-year-Buddy not to take the job he'd been offered. He and his wife are fine now. At least, according to her recent social media posts."

Peter stopped, looking at his food. He stood and packed his pasta container and utensils into the bag. "In fact, I can show you something that will help you. Let's go for a ride." Peter asked, half way to the front door, "Do you have time now?"

"I guess I do," Carrie replied. With him determined to leave, she doubted that she could get any work done until she saw what he had to show her. "I'll follow you in my car."

She turned off the coffee pot, tossed her Roselli's pasta into the refrigerator, and grabbed her keys. Minutes later, she was following Peter across town to his house.

When they arrived at Peter's, he threw his Roselli's bag into the fridge. "Not that good anyway," she heard him mumble.

He led Carrie downstairs to his office and through the secret panel into the time travel room. Opening a file drawer, he pulled out a copy he'd made of Carrie's handwritten note the night before. He held the paper out toward her.

Carrie froze. She thought of Peter handing her Mig's letter not-so-long ago. Her heart sunk, and tears threatened.

Peter seemed to guess what was going on with her. He placed the note on top of the file cabinet and stepped away.

Peter busied himself, straightening his collection of rocks and things, wiping dust off the shelf with his fingers, and adjusting the chair. Carrie saw him moving in her peripheral vision as she stared at the paper. She swallowed hard, then stepped forward and gingerly picked up the note.

Hearing the paper rustle as she retrieved it, Peter turned and stepped toward her. "Now, once you've read that note you wrote, walk into my office — if you like — and that piece of paper will go poof." He held his hands in the air and accentuated the *poof* with his fingers.

Carrie read, in her own handwriting, what she'd written about Buddy and the planned correction. Then, she walked to the time travel room's threshold. Looking down at the paper in her hand, she felt a sense of Déjà vu, almost. Except this time the note was in her handwriting instead of Mig's. Stepping forward, she watched the sparks of darkness remove the note from her hand, just as it had done with Mig's letter. The unpleasant scent filled the air, and she recognized it this time: rotten fruit.

"Let's sit down, Carrie," Peter said softly. Carrie did as he asked, taking a seat in the velvet chair facing his desk. Peter sat down in the chair behind his desk, folded his hands, and began explaining his trip.

"Part of this story, you read in your own note. I took a trip back to last year, to the day Buddy said was the day he'd gone on the interview and been offered the new job. His taking it would have led to a divorce. Just as we planned, I ran in to him as he was leaving his job interview and pretended I worked there."

Carrie heard the "we planned" and searched her mind for any memory of the conversation where she had helped Peter plan. She remembered nothing, which was disconcerting.

"I told Buddy I was working there and how much I hated it. Then, I stuck around for a while just to make sure that he was convinced not to take the job."

"Okay, I'm with you so far," Carrie said, though she wasn't sure she felt *with* anything. Feeling disoriented, she lowered her head onto her hands, her hair tumbling forward.

Peter continued, obliviously, "I checked Buddy and his wife out online this morning. No red flags. He's still listed as an employee at his current job, not the job he was offered. Job well done and — while I know it's tough for you to not remember — you were a good helper to me and made a difference to these people."

"Thank you," Carrie said from behind her hands.

She heard nothing for several minutes. Then, Peter asked, "Would you have preferred that I hadn't told you?"

She thought about that. It was unsettling to know that her memories of the past few days were, in some way, just fiction. *Well, not really*, she thought. *More like replacements.*

She lifted her head and looked at Peter. "I think at some point, I'll be glad that I know. Right now, though," she shrugged, "I kind of wish I didn't."

"Fair enough," Peter said.

Carrie thought that he looked worried. "I can handle it. God knows I've handled worse."

They sat silently. After a minute, Peter got up and left the room. Carrie heard him doing something noisy upstairs. He returned ten minutes later with tacos, and set a plate down in front of her. "To make up for that lousy pasta. And for not giving you time to eat it."

He opened the sliding door, stepped outside, and sat at the patio table to eat.

Carrie took a bite of taco. *Wow, surprisingly good. Spicy, too.* She ate slowly and focused on eating, stopping herself from thinking about anything else. She ate the last bite from her plate, took a breath, and relaxed.

Peter had finished eating, and was sitting with his back to her, looking toward his garden. She rose to join him on the patio. Stepping outside, the breeze ruffled her hair, and she drew in a deep breath of the fresh air. As she exhaled and dropped onto a chair, he asked, "Better?"

"Yes. Thank you for the food, Peter. It was delicious."

He nodded and looked out toward his garden again.

"When I was a child," Carrie said, "I took a pretty good hit on the head while I was out playing. The next day, I woke up and didn't remember anything about the previous evening... really, nothing past lunch. It was scary to me — to not remember getting hurt, or having dinner, or going to bed. My mother talked to me, explained what had happened, and she calm me down. That's kind of how I feel now — a little scared. A little confused."

Peter asked, "But your mom made you feel better?"

"Yeah," Carrie said. "Yes, she did."

Peter's eyes glazed briefly, then in a far-away voice, he said, "When I was a young man, I was living in this house, my grandfather's house. I stayed here and traveled with him."

Family money, Carrie thought, confirming her musing from her first visit.

"He's the one who set up the time-travel room," he continued, gesturing toward the secret panel and the now-hidden room, "but that's a part of the tale I'll save for another day. Maybe.

"My older brother, Simon, had died when he was 18. He's *one* of the reasons I am so focused on helping people. Just after we lost Simon, my Grampa let me in on his secret of being a time traveler.

"Of course, I wanted to go back and change things, to save my brother's life. My Grampa urged me not to do it. It would have been selfish, was what my Grampa said. I think there was more to it than that; but, he didn't elaborate. I trusted my Grampa, and followed his advice to let Simon go. It was hard, not bringing Simon back to us." He sighed, rubbing his eyes hard.

Carrie reached out and touched his hand. "I'm so sorry."

"Thank you." He tapped her hand in return before continuing. "A few years later, as I was becoming more experienced with time travel, I decided to correct one of my own regrets. I went back to Simon's funeral, and I hugged my mother and told her it would be all right. I hadn't been able to do that, originally. I ran out of the funeral without speaking to Mom. For years, I regretted not comforting her, but at that time I was caught up in my own pain."

Clearing his throat and taking a drink of coffee, he continued, "In the trip that I took to hug my mother, I waited until the young-Peter of that time ran out, and then I walked in — doing what my younger self had not done — and comforted my mother. If my mother noticed that I looked a bit older, she said nothing.

"I also stopped to talk with my grandfather... told him what I'd done. You see, past-me couldn't know what I'd done on my trip from the future, so Grampa needed to tell my younger self I'd come back, so that he... I... could let go of the regret for running out on Mom.

"There were never two versions of me in the room with my mother — though she would have understood; but, there were many other people there and any one of them might have been confounded by seeing two of me in the room, even with the age difference. We've kept our secret from most. Grampa told me, my mom and Grandma knew, and very, very few others. And you, now."

He turned his head and Carrie thought she saw him wipe at his eyes.

He looked toward her and said, "That time trip I took for myself, but also for my Mom. It helped both of us, and trust me, I understand how important it was to you to have your own mother comfort you. If there's anything I can do, things I can explain to help you get comfortable with time travel, just ask."

They sat on the patio in silence. Seeing Peter glance at his watch, Carrie noticed it was almost 3 o'clock. "Hey, I'm going to head out," she said. "I really should get back to work. Try to work, at least. I'm sure you have a lot going on too."

"Call me if you have any questions," was all Peter said. He waved as she left the patio and she walked around the side of the house to her car.

When Carrie arrived home, her head was filled with thoughts — of her mother, Peter's surprisingly personal tale, and her missing memories. After a brief attempt at working, she instead flopped down on the couch and turned on the television.

Ignoring the TV, Carrie zeroed in on the one thing affecting her right now — the days she'd lost, according to Peter, and her proximity to one of his corrections.

Knowing that her life had been altered and that she'd never remember helping Peter time travel, Carrie wasn't sure how to feel. The memories were not recoverable, he'd said. Only Peter would ever have memories from their apparent dinner at Roselli's. She felt fear creeping up on her, and attempted to assure herself. *Nothing bad happened. Probably. Yes, it's freaky but I can handle it.*

If she couldn't get a handle on her disorientation, how could she ever hope to learn about time travel? She wondered if it might vex her less over time, as she learned even more.

What if knowing is the hard part? She knew about the changes because Peter had told her about them; just as he had told her about her own death, which had sent her reeling. It was the knowing that caused her distress, she realized. *Is ignorance bliss?*

She chastised herself. *I want to know. Anyone would be over the moon to learn the ins-and-outs of time travel. I need to quit letting this missing-memories thing scare me.*

"This is what I asked for," she said out loud to the empty living room, "I want Peter to teach me more."

Not for the last time, she wished Mig was there. He would have embraced the chance to experience time travel alongside her, and he'd have made it more exciting, and less frightening. *He'd have loved this.*

14 – Baby Steps

Carrie's morning flew by. She'd finished half a pot of coffee, cleared waiting emails, and by noon she'd posted four articles to the news site and edited several drafts.

She was just considering what to make for lunch when her cell phone rang. It was Peter calling, she saw on the cell phone display, and she hesitated. It rang twice more before she convinced herself that she was ready to handle more time travel craziness, and she answered.

"Carrie, could you stop by later tonight?" Peter asked.

Carrie was speechless for a moment. *Does he ever slow down?* Then, she thought, *In for a penny, in for a pound*, and responded, "Yes, I can."

"Good. Park in the driveway and come in the patio door. How does 11 P.M. sound?"

Really late, she thought. She figured time didn't mean much to him, nor did social graces, and agreed, "I'll be there."

She made a mug of soup and sipped at it. Despite the distraction of the call, she found enough focus to finish two more articles, and made several phone calls — scheduling an interview with a business owner for the next day.

As she added the appointments to her calendar, she paused. *I wonder if there are any appointments I've missed without knowing, thanks to Peter Braggin.*

Probably not. But still...

***

Carrie arrived at Peter's house right on time, and walked around to the patio. Two small lights brightened the table area. The surrounding trees hovered in the darkness. Spotting two tea glasses on the patio table, she guessed that Peter wanted to talk outside. She stood in the light surrounding the table and waited.

Peter appeared a few minutes later and motioned for Carrie to sit down as he sat.

"Carrie, I'm going to hazard a guess that you're absorbing what I'm teaching you about time travel, but maybe struggling a little bit with the overall idea. Am I right?"

Carrie nodded. "Yes," she said, "that's just about how I'd put it."

He slapped his hand against the table, "Just as I'd figured. Okay, well, if you'll continue to trust me, I would like to have you stay inside while I take a trip tonight. I'm making a minor change, and I will do my best to make you as comfortable as possible."

Carrie thought of the disorienting loss of memories, she'd experienced by leaving the time travel room while Peter traveled for Buddy. This was a chance move past her fears, and she wouldn't lose memories. She had to do it. "I'll stay. I want to know more. It makes me nervous that you haven't said why or where you're going. What will I remember if I don't know how things...were...are?"

Peter laughed. "I promise that if you stay in this room, you'll remember everything tomorrow. You'll have memories of what originally happened, and know what I've corrected."

Suddenly, Carrie understood why he'd set their meeting late at night. He'd wanted her to be as tired as possible. She *was* tired when she'd arrived, but the idea of watching time change had perked her up.

"I'll give it a shot."

"Excellent! Drink your tea, maybe make a run to the rest room, and I'll meet you in there."

Carrie did exactly as suggested. When she walked through the panel, Peter was seated in the wooden chair.

"Please shut the panel and settle in over there, out of my line of sight. The pillow and blanket are there in the corner--" he pointed to the space next to the file cabinets, "and when I go on my trip, try to go to sleep. It's late enough that I hope that won't be too difficult for you, despite the close quarters. And do not leave the room or you'll forget again."

"I won't leave the room."

"I'm glad to hear that, Carrie. Once I've gone, you sleep, and you'll wake up in your own bed tomorrow morning." He looked at her intently, paternally. "Come and see me tomorrow when you can, and I'll tell you what I've done, and we'll talk about your memories. I promise *this* will not be as jarring as when you couldn't remember. All right?"

Carrie breathed a sigh of relief. She trusted him already, she found. "All right."

Peter sat down on the wooden chair, took a deep breath, and before her eyes, thousands of black flashes began. They looked like fireworks, but made of black. A flurry of them covered Peter; then the flashing stopped and the room was lit only by the overhead light.

The chair was empty. Peter had gone.

Carrie whooshed out a long breath, and when she inhaled, she found the air smelled of freshness. It reminded her of holding her babies as she rocked them, and it calmed her.

Carrie wrapped herself in the blanket Peter had left for her. Fluffing the pillow against a file cabinet, she closed her eyes, not wanting to see the empty chair. She willed herself to go to sleep, breathing in the sweet scent. A minute later, she became incredibly sleepy, and after a light-headed moment, she was out.

The cell phone ringing awoke Carrie at 8 A.M. She reached for the phone and tried to read the caller's name. Only one of her eyes had opened. Peering sideways at the phone, she saw it was Peter and answered.

After greeting her, Peter launched into an explanation of his trip. He told Carrie that he had gone back to the date she had given him for when the horse at the therapy farm had been attacked by the dog. All he had done was phone the farm, tell the woman who answered that a stray dog had been spotted, that he was a neighbor (he had lied), and warned the woman to keep the horses inside. He'd also called animal control and let them know a stray dog had been spotted near the horse farm.

Shocked, Carrie said, I'll call you back," and ended the call. She immediately called Rosa at the farm. Trying to be nonchalant, Carrie asked Rosa if she'd seen the stray dog that was supposed to be loose in the area. Rosa said not recently, but that she remembered getting a call about a stray weeks ago and her husband had later mentioned that he'd seen animal control pick up a dog.

After a few minutes questioning Rosa and chatting, Carrie ended the call, stunned.

She called Peter back. "Baby Girl is fine," she said, incredulous. "Thank you!" She and Peter spoke briefly, and she thanked him again before ending the call.

In Carrie's mind, parts of what Peter had taught her began to click into place. Her memories of seeing Baby Girl injured were faded, almost dream-like. Having such a tangible result from his time travel, she finally understand.

She checked the news site from her laptop. She saw that the article she'd written on the dog attack was now an article on the farm's new barn, with a photo of a healthy Baby Girl standing tall next to Rosa.

She remembered writing *both* articles.

After Carrie ended the phone call, Peter smiled, pleased that he'd made the trip to save the horse. Making time travel personal could only help Carrie understand what he'd been teaching her.

Peter's thoughts shifted to a dog he had briefly-owned, and named Max. He chuckled, remembering how the dog had trotted around the yard with him on the day he'd brought Max home from the shelter.

Peter hadn't told Carrie, but on the trip that he'd taken to avert the dog attack on the horse, Baby Girl, Peter had gone by the animal shelter to see the dog that animal control had picked up at the farm. He'd had been shocked to discover that the dog was Max. Not only had Max escaped and become Peter's dog, briefly, but Max had escaped again and chased the horse — at least, until Peter took his trip to save Baby Girl.

When Peter had approached Max at the shelter, he could have sworn that the dog had recognized him. That was impossible, as the dog could not know him, having never been his pet on the timeline now.

It concerned Peter that he'd encountered the same dog on two unrelated trips. Sure, he'd seen some of the same people and places on different trips. While his experience had shown how people reacted to time changes, Max's reaction had him thinking that animals might be an unknown variable.

Peter hoped that he was ascribing too much meaning to it; but, he considered the idea that, at some point, he might research the effect of time travel on dogs.

That evening, Carrie didn't feel up to cooking just for herself and ate cereal for dinner. She thought of Peter showing up at her door with pasta. Thinking how many years he had taken his meals alone, she pitied him, which made her more grateful for the years she and the kids had spent with Mig.

Feeling calmer than she had for days, she thought about Mig, and how he had spent time with Peter before writing her that letter. Carrie understood Mig's concerns better now. From what she'd seen, time travel was a complex, mysterious tool.

She wished Mig hadn't made Peter promise not to help her; but, she knew Mig, and guessed that he had done it to protect her.

15 – Time Stalker

Carrie stepped out of her house, locked the door, and yawned. She felt drained today — another tough day. Early this morning, she'd yelled to tell Mig that the coffee was ready before recalling that he wasn't there anymore.

It had taken all her will to get ready for work and out the door. As she climbed into her car, she noticed a black SUV parked and running in front of a neighbor's house. She figured the neighbor must have a visitor, waved as she went by, and gave it no more thought. She had errands to run that would likely take her all day, including an interview with a shop owner at noon.

Leaving a downtown coffee shop with a hot travel mug of latte, Carrie walked toward her car, passing a black SUV on her way. For a moment, she thought it was the one that had been at her neighbor's house earlier, but she dismissed the idea. *There must be dozens of black SUVs around town*, she thought. Still, she made a mental note of the license plate number before driving away.

After errands and a quick stop for lunch, Carrie arrived at her scheduled interview with the owner of a new antique shop just outside downtown. Speaking with the shop owner, she filled two pages with notes, took a few photos, bid the owner good-bye, and decided to head home right away to prepare the article.

Approaching her car, she noticed a black SUV. It was parked on the opposite side of the street, the engine running. She walked toward her car, trying to nonchalantly check the license plate. It was the same number as she'd seen earlier.

She stopped, peering at the driver's window, but couldn't see through the tint. The little hairs stood up on the back of her neck. It could be a coincidence, but it rattled her. She stared at the vehicle, unable to move. Then, she heard the engine rev and the SUV pulled away.

When it disappeared down the street, she became able to move again. She hurried to her car and drove home, taking care to use the highway — less time on lonely back roads — although she doubted anyone would be looking to do her harm.

No SUV followed her home. When she arrived, Carrie hurried inside, locked the door, and closed the blinds. She sat down in the living room, listening for any noises around the house. Occasionally, she peeked through the blinds.

After a while, Carrie calmed and sat down to write the article on the new shop. She stayed home to work the rest of the afternoon, leaving her remaining errands undone.

The next day, a Wednesday, Carrie checked the street before running to her car. She had places to go and couldn't just hide inside. *I probably overreacted. There wasn't any reason for someone to follow me. Obviously, it had just been coincidence — someone else running similar errands.*

That thought calmed her and she went about her business. The day was uneventful.

The next day was, too.

By Friday, Carrie had stopped watching for the SUV. She interviewed the local Chamber director and a ghost hunter from the next town over. It was a productive morning, and as she drove home through downtown Hope Wells, she stopped for coffee.

Then, as she walked out of the shop with a newly purchased latte, she saw the black SUV. It was parked across the street. This time, it wasn't running. Without warning, a man appeared at her side, startling her.

He was barely taller than she, well-dressed but heavyset, with combed-back light hair and squinting eyes. He was wearing a smile, but it was as false as the knock-off watch on his wrist. His smile widening, he asked, "You're Carrie Weathers, aren't you?"

Carrie nodded. She stepped backward to put more space between them. He stepped forward and closed the gap she'd made. He was so close that she could smell his cologne; it seemed cheap and from the reek Carrie thought he must have slathered it on. She sneezed, taking another step away. Again, the man closed the space between them.

"I've been hoping to talk with you," he said in a voice that almost sounded friendly but failed. "I read your article a few weeks ago about a local scientist, a Peter Braggin. Great stuff."

"Thank you," Carrie managed to say.

"Well," he continued, puffing out his chest, "I'm Vincent Duke. Maybe you've seen my real estate ads around town?" He gestured toward a public bench nearby with his name, number, and a photograph — one that was either old or retouched to make him appear thinner and tanned. Carrie could see that he was exceptionally pale, and she doubted the tan in the picture was natural.

"Yes, of course," Carrie said, trying not to sound unfriendly. She reached out and shook his hand briefly; it was clammy and wet. "I have seen them. Nice to meet you, Mr. Duke," she lied.

"Call me Vinnie," he said, smiling creepily.

"Vinnie," she said. "I'm glad that you liked the article. I appreciate you being one of our readers." His eyes seemed stuck in a perpetual squint. She suspected he was intentionally hiding his eyes.

He took a deep breath, showed his teeth again, and asked, "So, do you know Peter Braggin well?"

His asking about Peter made her uneasy. Proceeding with caution, she answered, "Oh, we've interviewed him a time or two for the paper. Nice man." She smiled as genuinely as she could manage, "Odd, but nice," she added, allowing a hint of truth.

Her discomfort grew as Vinnie laughed. There was nothing funny about the laugh and Carrie tensed.

"Yes, yes. Peter Braggin is an odd duck." He pursed his lips after saying this. They whitened even more than his pale face.

Carrie tried to change the subject. "So, um, Vinnie, are you interested in advertising with our newspaper?"

He stared at her, his already squinted eyes turned to slits as he frowned. Carrie felt glad that she had a true reason for seeing Peter Braggin, as she was not a good liar. If she'd had to make something up, she feared this scary man would have seen right through her. As it was, his expression made her think he wasn't buying what she was selling. The hairs on the back of her neck prickled again. What little Carrie could see of his eyes looked dark and seemed to have no shine to them.

She fished her business card out of her pocket, taking another step away as she held up the card. He didn't take it, which was fine with her. It had only been an excuse for her to move back, and she was relieved when he didn't step forward this time. He continued staring.

Meeting his uncomfortable gaze, Carrie said, "You know, I'll bet that you have some interesting stories as a real estate agent. Maybe one of your experiences would be of interest to our readers--" She stopped, swallowing hard, as he glowered at her, his jaw working as if he was grinding his teeth.

"So," Vinnie said as if he hadn't heard her, "What other business do you have with Peter Braggin?"

"None," she said quickly, then added, "though he did say he might run an ad." Her voice broke, and she knew the slight tremble had given away her lie.

Vinnie's face began to redden. Seeing his anger, Carrie tried to change the subject, "Listen, would you be interested in being interviewed about any unusual listings you've had, any haunted houses or weird finds?" Carrie had no intention of interviewing him. She looked around to see how far she was from her car.

He raised an eyebrow, "No. No haunted houses." Suddenly, Vinnie reached out and gripped her arm. Carrie jumped with surprise and tried to pull away. His grip tightened.

"I imagine you and Peter Braggin have had some interesting talks," he sneered.

"Interviews," she corrected him. She pulled again, and he squeezed hard before releasing her arm. Carrie's coffee fell from her hand, splashing over her shoes and the sidewalk. She stepped backward away from Vinnie, rubbing at her now-sore forearm. "What are you doing, Mr. Duke?" She yelled loud enough that she saw heads turn inside the coffee shop.

He glared at her, turned, and briskly walked to his SUV.

Carrie was inside her car and locking the door seconds later. She drove straight home.

Carrie locked all her house's doors and windows. She wanted to call the police but didn't. Instead, she stood at the front window, peering out at the street through the blinds.

What do I do? With no other ideas, she made a pot of coffee, her hands shaking. Then, she moved one of the tall chairs from the kitchen to the living room, positioning it so she could easily see out the edge of the blinds. She held the mug of coffee for twenty minutes without taking a drink, watching.

When it was too dark to see, she walked around the house turning on the outside lights. She tossed a container of leftovers into the microwave and poured two fresh mugs of coffee. She set the second cup on the counter, wishing Mig was there to drink his. Then she sipped at her coffee until the microwave beeped.

Eating dinner away from the windows helped her to relax, a little. She'd seen no black SUV go by. Part of her thought that she should call the police. But, she was afraid of answering questions that the police might ask. After all, she didn't know this man Vincent Duke, and trying to explain his coming after her because of a time traveler she knew was a conversation she did not want to have.

I need to do something, she thought. At the very least, she knew that she needed to let Peter know what had happened. She should have called him right away, and would have if she hadn't been so afraid.

She picked up her cell phone, then set it down, deciding to send Peter an email instead of calling. She kept it short. "Met your friend Vincent Duke today," it read. She hit Send, and heard the familiar *swoosh* as it sent.

Before she could even touch the keyboard again, her cell phone rang. "Are you all right?" were the first words out of Peter's mouth.

"Yes, I'm okay." She proceeded to tell him how Vincent Duke had approached her, how strained the conversation had been, and how Vinnie had grabbed hold of her before leaving.

Through the phone, Carrie could hear the anger in Peter's response, "I'll take care of him."

They talked for a few more seconds, Peter promising he'd call her again soon, and he ended the call.

Carrie wanted to stop thinking about her exchange with Vincent Duke. Although she trusted that Peter would, somehow, take care of Mr. Duke, she missed Mig being there to have her back. They'd always had each other's back. Right now, she didn't feel safe alone, the house far too quiet.

Carrie sat at her computer, staring at the screen, trying to distract herself by making a to-do list. When that didn't work, she pushed herself through her notes from the day's interviews — before Mr. Duke's interruption — and drafted articles on the Chamber and the ghost hunter. It was a struggle, but by midnight, she managed to finish the drafts, and an entire pot of coffee.

Carrie closed her laptop, checked the door locks umpteen times, and shuffled off to the bedroom. After going through her nighttime routine, she draped her injured arm across Mig's space on the bed, remembering how easy it had been to fall asleep when he was there with her. She brushed aside all other thoughts, and sunk deep into her imagination. Picturing him beside her, she drifted off to sleep, cheeks wet — as was the new normal.

First thing the next morning, Carrie took a good look at her sore arm. There were dark bruises where Vincent Duke had grabbed her the day before. She touched her wrist and winced. It seemed to look worse as she showered, the water accentuating the colors in the bruises. She dressed, and tenderly applied lotion before deciding to wear a long-sleeved shirt.

Peter called mid-morning, asking to meet her for lunch at a restaurant several towns over. She liked his idea of meeting far away.

The restaurant was a good fifty-minute drive for Carrie. She could have made the trip in half-an-hour, but she kept exiting the highway and getting back on, hoping her slightly ridiculous, and certainly amateurish, evasion technique would be enough to keep Vincent Duke from following her. She didn't know what his problem was, but she knew it wouldn't be good for him to see her and Peter at lunch together.

Carrie and Peter arrived at the restaurant at the same time. She guessed that he'd probably been doing some circuitous driving too, a suspicion Peter later confirmed. They sat at a table in the back and ordered barbecue plates. The restaurant was a hole-in-the-wall but known for its award-winning Carolina-style barbecue.

Peter started the conversation, "Let me bring you up-to-speed on my pal Vincent Duke." He laughed, but the laugh sounded hollow to Carrie. She didn't think Vinnie's demeanor was funny either.

Peter explained that his trouble with Vinnie had started when Peter refused to help him; in fact, Peter denied he was able to time travel.

Vinnie was a middle-class, entitled man who thought way more of himself than he should have. "He showed up at my house, asking me to go back in time and ensure he became a wealthy man. I read his intentions easily. Very bad intentions."

It must have been really easy for Peter. Even I could see Vinnie was up to no good, Carrie thought.

"The man was practically drooling to be rich," Peter added.

Vinnie's sad story centered around his belief that his birthright had been stolen from him. He had been raised rich. Now he was living a comfortable life, but it wasn't enough. He said that he deserved the extravagant life he'd lived as a child, and as a young man.

"Vinnie told me his family had cheated him. When his parents had died, all their money went to his half-brother, which Vinnie insisted was due to his father's favoritism. Now Vinnie works as a real estate agent--"

I've seen his ads around town. He made a point of showing me one of them," Carrie interrupted.

"Yes, I've seen them, too. Well, he thinks he's supposed to be more than he is. He insisted that he should have received the inheritance instead."

Following his conversation with Vinnie, Peter had researched the man and his family. Peter found information on multiple awards for charity work that Vinnie's half-brother, Richard, had received. "I got the impression that Richard had worked hard, behaved charitably, and carefully tended the inheritance. He owns several homes, which probably fuels Vinnie's jealousy.

"Meanwhile, Vinnie has filed bankruptcy. Various lawsuits against him say, to me, that Vinnie has alienated many business associates. He hasn't sold all that much real estate, either. He might make a few sales using bullying and pressure, but the guy has no savvy."

Peter sighed. "Vinnie is kind of an ass — excuse my language — and his bad attitude likely contributes to his failures. He's the cause of his own problems, though he's been trying to push the blame onto Richard, and now on to me. I thought he was just a blow-hard, and I didn't realize until he confronted you just how far he would go to get my attention."

"So, he's mad at you, and came for me to try and change your mind?"

"I think so. And I'm sorry, Carrie. You know, it was pure happenstance that I met him," Peter said, shaking his head. "My next-door neighbor put his house up for sale. I didn't know Vinnie until the day he came to post the For Sale sign at my neighbor's. One minute I'm digging in my garden, and the next, this guy in a suit is crashing through my bushes from the neighbor's yard. He caught me by surprise.

"He introduced himself and explained that he was going to sell my neighbor's house. He went on and on. I listened politely. He gushed about how huge my house was and how he could sell it for me. I declined, but he was a pushy S.O.B. We didn't part on the best of terms.

"Well, a couple of days later, he calls and wants to meet with me. I figured he wanted to talk about my house again and told him I wasn't selling. That's when he says my work looks interesting, and he has a proposition for me. At that point, I figured out that he had looked me up online, and knowing what an aggravating guy he was, I needed to put him off. I agreed to meet — out on the patio — that afternoon and I went with my craziest persona to try to get rid of him. Gave it my best shot, really."

He shrugged, then continued, "Unlike so many of the folks I've met who had less-than-honorable intentions, Vinnie didn't buy my act. He said he could see right through me and knew my time travel 'hullaballoo' was the real deal. That's the word he used.

"Sometimes liars are better at recognizing other liars for who they really are, or at recognizing a lie when they hear it. If I hadn't been ambushed in my backyard, and caught unawares, he might never have looked me up online.

"Anyway, he told me that I was wrong to refuse him. He acted like he was entitled to my help, and I was withholding it... like a little kid demanding a toy after mommy takes it away."

"He seemed pretty unhinged to me," Carrie interjected.

Peter nodded furiously. "From that meeting forward, Vinnie kept after me. He called me multiple times and explained his 'tale of woe' of not being rich enough, etcetera, and how he deserved my help. He offered me riches if I helped him get his.

"I should have seen earlier that he was not just a fool but also calculating. I should have gone back to fix that first meeting. Unfortunately for both of us, I underestimated him. I'm sorry that it's reached this point, Carrie. I will correct it."

Their food arrived, and they both thanked the server.

In a low voice, Peter said, "Vinnie called me again today as I was leaving the house to meet you. He suggested I either travel back in time and force Vinnie's father to change his will, or I go back and kill Richard before their parents died."

Carrie knew that Peter would not do either of these things. He focused on fixing people's pain. But Vinnie's supposed *pain* came from a misbegotten belief that he deserves everything that he wanted.

"The pain of a rich person wanting to be richer is not real pain," Peter said, shaking his head. "Even suggesting I kill someone for him, a family member no less..."

They both shook their heads at this. Peter took a brief break from the story and ate a bite of his now-tepid barbecue. He finished off a few hush-puppies and resumed.

"Obviously," Peter told Carrie, "I won't carry out either of Vinnie's suggestions. I don't like him and I don't plan to help him at all. I knew it wouldn't get through to him, but I spent several minutes explaining the virtue of hard work. Vinnie cut me off. Then, he mentioned you in passing, which I took as a threat, and I hung up on him."

Carrie dropped her fork.

"In hindsight," Peter said, "I'm glad that I met him outside on the patio that day. I'm not quite sure what would have happened if I'd let him into my house. If he's as dangerous as I now believe him to be, Vinnie might have felt there was enough privacy to attack me, and my screams would have been muffled."

Carrie swallowed the barbecue she'd been chewing and stared at Peter. She hoped he was exaggerating. The bruises on her wrist suggested he wasn't.

"I should have figured out even then that he was no good. Especially given the way he figured *me* out, I should have known."

Peter had seen people like Vinnie before, he told Carrie, although until Vinnie came along, Peter had been able to figure each of them out and send them on their way. "Men seeking wealth — and it is usually men — never understand why their desire to be wealthier isn't of interest to me. They offer money and question my refusal. They can't see past their own pocketbook, nor the end of their nose." Peter rubbed his forehead. "Usually they give up. Vinnie isn't giving up."

Carrie knew the type of attitude Peter was describing. She'd met the occasional person who had no interests other than their own, even if it caused harm to others.

"Carrie," Peter said seriously, "I've dealt with many people over the years, but the anger that I think is in Vinnie is bigger, burning hotter, than anyone I've dealt with before. I'll come up with a solution as quickly as I can."

"You aren't going to help him, are you?" Carrie asked.

"No, of course I won't," Peter said. "And if you want to call the police, I understand completely. Keep in mind that when I travel to handle this guy, whatever the police do now will be undone."

Carrie leaned back in her chair and crossed her arms. She winced as she accidentally pushed down on her bruise.

"Can I see?" Peter asked.

Carrie saw his concern, and she rolled up her sleeve to show him the bruises on her arm. His eyes widened when he saw them, and she tugged her sleeve down to hide them again.

Peter sighed and continued, "Your encounter with Vinnie won't happen if I correct things the right way. I've got to set a plan, and take a trip and stop him before he escalates."

Carrie knew Peter was right. She wanted Vinnie to be stopped, punished even. She rubbed the bridge of her nose, thinking, then said, "No police. I get it. But I'm mad and I want to do *something*. If he's done this to me when I was trying to be nice, I can't imagine what he's done to people who he thinks have provoked him. Not that you did... but..." She took a deep breath. "What can I do to help you? How can we remove Vinnie's obsession with you — maybe with both of us?"

Carrie's anxiety level rose. *How do you stop a madman?*

Peter asked, "Do you have any ideas? I have a few possibilities in mind, but would like to hear your thoughts."

Carrie knew that Peter was frustrated because he wasn't able to avoid meeting Vinnie in the first place. "You have more experience with this than me, but would the easiest solution be to go back to the beginning, when he ambushed you in your garden?"

Peter angled his head side to side in a maybe-yes-maybe-no gesture. "Possibly, but that might be better as our backup plan. I'm thinking that I need to get to Vinnie before then. I need to make sure I get him handled, and in a way he can't happen upon me later. What I really need is to keep that guy from ever getting in the neighborhood, so he can never show up in my backyard.

"What if I...we... find a way to keep my neighbor from listing his house for sale with Vinnie? I need to sort out the details, maybe have a conversation with my neighbor, and I need to do it quickly. What do you think about that?"

She answered Peter, trying hard to keep her voice steady. "Sounds good to me, except you have other neighbors, Peter. And we may not be the only ones he's treating like this. How far do you think we should go to stop him? Not, I don't mean kill him, but maybe he's guilty of something we could use to... make sure he's punished?"

"That's an idea worth exploring. I need to think this through carefully," Peter said, "I can tell you're worried. I'm sure I can set things right. If you're done eating, though, we should probably leave. Go directly home if you can, Carrie. This out-of-town lunch may have kept him from seeing you with me, but he's still out there. Please let me know when you get home."

Carrie called Peter when she arrived at home, confirming that she was safely locked inside. He promised he'd call her the next day, and that Vinnie wouldn't be a problem much longer.

As if an afterthought, Peter asked Carrie to see if she could find out more about Vinnie's background, and any possibly shady business dealings. Before ending the phone call, Peter told her that he'd seen no sign of Vinnie, and assured her all would be corrected soon. The confident tone in Peter's voice, more than anything, gave comfort to Carrie.

She was beginning to understand the power that Peter had. He could rule the world, probably, if he set his mind to it. Instead, he chose to behave like a social worker or therapist and help others. *Mig would have really liked Peter*, she thought.

Then it dawned on her that Mig and Peter had met, in some previous form of the timeline. Mig probably *had* liked Peter. Maybe she'd ask the time traveler more about that, some day.

16 – SOS

Later that evening, Carrie was just sitting down to eat microwaved leftovers when she received a strange text message, "SOS P.H."

Although she didn't recognize the number it came from, she knew it was from Peter, even though he had always sent emails, not texts. *My grandfather called me P.H.*, she remembered him saying. She also recognized *SOS*. She and Mig used walkie-talkies when they traveled with the family in two vehicles, and they had taught the children some Morse Code. SOS was the call for help.

A ping announced a new text's arrival. From the same number, this text was just an address. She punched it into her navigation app and saw it was less than ten minutes away. She ran to her car.

Carrie drove to the address, parked nearby on Main Street, and exited her car. She scanned the few businesses with lights on, including a bar and a laundromat. Seeing no movement, she tried to figure out where Peter might be. The laundromat looked empty. The bar at the end of the block didn't seem likely. She was about to call Peter, when she spotted his car parked down an alley and sprinted toward it.

Just as she reached his car, she heard a whisper. *Someone called my name*. For one heartbeat, she feared that she might have just walked into a trap, that Vincent Duke was hiding in the shadows. Then she heard her name again and recognized Peter's voice.

"Where are you?" she whispered, peering around in the low light of the alley.

"Here, by the dumpster," Peter said. His voice sounded strained. She saw nothing but walked toward the dumpster. A car drove by the adjoining street and in the slight glow from its headlights, Carrie saw Peter seated on the ground next to the dumpster. She ran to him, kneeling and grabbing him by both arms.

She tried to lift him. No luck. Peter grunted and slid one foot under him. Carrie pulled steadily, and Peter was able to stand up.

They walked to the laundromat, Carrie supporting Peter. As they entered the well-lit space, Carrie looked him over. There was blood on his shirt and filth all over the back of his pants and jacket. She saw at least one dirty footprint on his side where he had been kicked.

Peter took a few steps forward toward a chair and Carrie helped him to sit. "That's lucky," he said. "There's no one here doing laundry. Got a quarter?"

"Are you serious?" Carrie yelled. She took a breath and lowered her voice, "What's going on?"

Peter looked at Carrie, "Thank you for coming. This is unfortunately the work of our friend Vinnie."

Carrie started to speak but Peter cut her off. "Please get me some water, a soda, anything. I'll tell you all about my dumb-ass mistake but right now I'm just really thirsty."

Carrie fished a couple singles out of her pocket. There was a row of vending machines at the back past the washers and dryers. She bought Peter a bottle of water and took it back to him. Then, she waited as he sipped the water and rested a bit.

She checked out the front window a couple of times, afraid that she'd see Vinnie coming toward them. The street was empty.

"He won't come back tonight," Peter said. She looked away from the door and toward Peter. He looked awful.

"He tricked me," Peter said, sounding embarrassed. "I received a text message that looked like it came from you."

Carries face turned red. Peter saw her and shook his head. "It was a text asking me to meet you at that bar down there, that you needed to talk to me right away." He motioned toward the bar at the end of the block. "I should have known it was a trick; you've never sent me any text. I should have called you to double-check."

"What did Vinnie do to you?"

"When I parked, Vinnie and some big dude with him jumped into my car and forced me to drive down the alley. Son of a-- I mean, Vinnie, he had a gun. He got the best of me today. I guess I'm lucky he only brought a guy with him to beat me up. He could have shot me."

"Oh, my gosh," Carrie exclaimed. "We should get you to a hospital."

"No, no hospital," Peter said, shaking his head. "I would appreciate if you could drive me somewhere, though. I've a friend who's a doctor, and he'll fix me up. The last thing I want to do is draw attention to myself, and any doctor would want to know why I was beaten. I'm not going to even try to explain that."

Carrie half-carried Peter to her car and lowered him into the passenger seat. She ran to the driver's side and climbed behind the wheel.

Peter directed her where to go. As she drove, he explained how he'd ended up by the dumpster.

Peter had decided to talk to Vinnie one more time. He knew the arrogant man wouldn't listen to him, but he wanted to try. "Mostly," he admitted, "I wanted to give Vinnie one last chance to be a decent human being. My mistake," Peter said. He hit the car door with the side of his fist, then howled in pain.

"Take it easy. Where do I turn next?"

"Up a mile, then right."

After she made the turn, he gave her the next street name for a right turn, and continued his story.

He'd gone to Vinnie's house. Even the house looked pompous, he told Carrie, chuckling. Vinnie had let him in, and immediately began talking about how he was glad Peter had come to his senses, and how they should get started right away.

Peter had cut him off. He'd firmly told Vinnie that not only would he not help him, but it was in Vinnie's best interests to leave Carrie and Peter alone, or he might just find himself an even poorer man when he woke up in the morning.

"At that point, Vinnie turned almost purple with rage. He was getting desperate, and I saw it. When Vinnie threatened to go to the authorities and tell them about my ability to travel through time, I told Vinnie, 'good luck with that' and I laughed at him."

Peter sighed, and said to Carrie. "Also a mistake. I should have been smarter about it, but the guy just... he just... and threatening you... I was so..." he trailed off.

"Okay. It's okay. I get it." She hit her blinker and made the turn.

"Next left, there," Peter said pointing. He released a long, drawn out sigh. "I don't know. I thought I could push back hard, and he'd fold. Turns out, he's the most deranged person I've ever met. Live and learn."

"Good lord, Peter," Carrie said, trying to stay focused on the road.

Peter pointed for her to take the next turn, then said, "I left his house, but a little while later I received the text that I thought was from you. After our secret-agent style lunch, I was concerned. I guess after I'd left, Vinnie set up the ruse to draw me to town. Thank goodness he hadn't taken my phone when he dumped me. Or, you know, killed me."

Carrie gripped the steering wheel so hard her knuckles whitened. "Yeah, I'm glad about that, too. You're not gonna try to reason with him again, right? Time travel time now?"

"Yep," Peter said, sighing again. After a moment, he said, "I really appreciate your coming for me."

"No problem," Carrie said, feeling sick. She was thankful Peter hadn't been killed, but their situation wasn't any closer to being corrected.

Peter's brown skin whitened, the blood drained from his face. "Oh Lord, Carrie! I'm so glad he came for me and not you. I'm glad you're all right. This Vinnie has me off my game, and it could have been much worse if he'd come after you tonight."

Carrie shivered at the thought, unconsciously locking the car doors again. They rode on in silence for several minutes.

Peter pointed to an intersection coming up, "Turn left at this next light. We're almost there." He then directed Carrie to pull into the driveway of an expansive Victorian home. Carrie recognized it; they were not far from Peter's home.

As soon as Peter knocked on the front door, a man in a bathrobe opened it. He recognized Peter, and invited them both inside. The man saw that Peter was injured, and helped Carrie move Peter to a couch.

Peter thanked him and said, "Dr. Lopez, this is Carrie. She's a reporter... and a friend."

"A reporter." Dr. Lopez repeated. "Are you writing a story about Peter? What's going on? How'd he get hurt?"

"I, uh..." Carrie wasn't sure how to answer. Then she looked at Peter. She didn't know who this doctor-friend was, how much he knew, or what she should — or shouldn't — say to him.

"Doc, Carrie's been helping me at my travel agency," Peter said. Carrie saw him wink at Dr. Lopez, who grinned.

"Ah," Dr. Lopez said to Carrie, "welcome to the amazing travels of the mysterious Peter B." To Peter, he said, "Let's see what the damage is, my friend. Hopefully nothing is broken this time."

"This time?" Carrie asked. "How many times has Peter come here for medical care?"

The doctor laughed heartily, "I have no idea. Who knows how many times he's come here and then wiped my memory after, right, Peter?"

"Never," Peter said, then winked at Carrie.

Carrie sat down, letting her head fall back against the couch cushion, and wished for it all to be over soon.

She watched while the doctor gave Peter a once-over. When he was sure nothing was broken, and Peter didn't look too terribly bloody, the doctor sent him into his guest room for a shower. Dr. Lopez gathered clean clothes and tossed them in after Peter, then returned to the living room and sat down opposite Carrie.

"More things in heaven and earth, thanks to our Peter Horacio, am I right?" Dr. Lopez asked Carrie. His expression was grim, despite the humor in his words. "It is nice to meet another member of Mr. B's exclusive club."

Carrie nodded. "Yes, I guess it is. It's nice to meet you, doctor. How do you know Peter?"

The doctor leaned back against the couch and sighed. "Well," he said, looking up at the ceiling, "I met the inimitable Mr. B more than a decade ago. I actually met Peter and his grandfather after they had a fight, of sorts." He smirked. "I became a member of the traveler's club after pulling a musket ball out of Alfonso's — his grandfather's — leg. Lucky me."

"Good lord," exclaimed Carrie. "A musket ball?"

"Yes, a musket ball," Dr. Lopez confirmed. "I just happened to be out walking my dog — down there near Mr. B's house — and saw him helping his grandfather into his car. I could see the blood covering his pant leg and offered to help.

"Now," he said, shrugging his shoulders, "I am the official doctor for the Mr. B travel agency." He laughed at his own joke. Carrie forced herself to laugh along with him.

When Peter emerged from the guest room, showered and looking much better, she noticed him listing to one side.

The clothes he'd put on were too big for him. His shirt was open, but the doctor opened it wider and pressed along Peter's ribs. "Were you punched or kicked here?" Dr. Lopez asked.

"Yes," Peter said, his voice strained. Carrie could see the pain on Peter's face each time the doctor prodded him.

Dr. Lopez stepped back and shook his finger at Peter, "Okay, Mr. B, I am ninety percent sure nothing is broken. I don't have magical eyesight to see through you, though. There could be a fracture, even internal bleeding. You want to take a ride with me to the hospital?"

Peter shook his head, "No, but thank you for asking." The doctor threw his hands up and looked skyward in mock exasperation. Or maybe it was real exasperation. Carrie wasn't quite sure.

Peter slowly sat down on the couch. Dr. Lopez settled into a chair opposite Carrie. "Thank you for helping me, Doc," Peter said. "Again, you've come through for me, dear friend."

The doctor waved off the thanks. "Drop by any time, Peter. Maybe next time, visit when you don't need medical help. We'll raise a glass to your grandfather. Perhaps Carrie will join us, if you haven't left her on a battlefield somewhere by then." He winked at Carrie.

Peter winced. "Not fair, doc. My grandfather took that trip on his own. I played no part in his foray into the Revolutionary War."

Both men laughed. Carrie forced a laugh, not really feeling the topic to be funny at all.

"Well, if you won't go to the hospital, you're staying here where I can keep an eye on you," Dr. Lopez said firmly.

Peter agreed to stay the night without further argument, putting his arms up in mock surrender, which must have hurt, as he quickly wrapped his hand over his ribs.

Carrie asked if she could stay on the couch and the doctor acquiesced.

Several times in the night, she was awakened by Dr. Lopez moving around, checking on Peter, and she was glad that he'd agreed to stay.

Peter turned over in the bed, his injuries made more uncomfortable by his being in an unfamiliar bed. He felt exposed being away from his home, his time travel room; and it concerned him that, in addition to Carrie, he'd now potentially exposed Dr. Lopez to danger.

He knew Carrie had stayed, rather than going home. *To her empty home*, Peter thought, then wondered where the thought had come from. Dr. Lopez had given him several capsules to take, they were taking away the pain already, and he wondered if they were impacting his thinking.

He found himself reviewing his time with Mig. He'd liked Mig right away when they'd met at the expo. When Mig came to see Peter after Carrie died, they had sat drinking coffee and conversing like old friends. Peter had told Mig about what he did, much as Peter had confessed to Carrie on her first visit to his house.

When Mig asked Peter if he would bring his wife back, it had been an easy decision. Peter had agreed immediately. Still, he met with Mig several more times, enjoying their conversations about time travel, and inviting Mig help him with one of his corrections, just as he'd done with Carrie.

Yes, he'd liked Mig. They'd had much in common, and discovered they'd grown up in similar households. Many of their life experiences, good and bad, were alike, despite their age difference.

Thinking of their conversations made him miss Mig's friendship; something that he thought he should have shared with Carrie.

After Peter took a trip to, anonymously, advise past-Mig to keep past-Carrie at home — ensuring she avoided the car accident that had killed her, Peter had missed Mig's company. He'd also felt guilty.

Peter hadn't told Carrie everything. He had shown her Mig's letter, but he hadn't described to her how torn Mig was between his spiritual views and using time travel to bring her back. Peter and Mig had spent long hours discussing this. Mig felt unsure where time travel fit in when it came to death, and he had concerns that if Peter brought Carrie back, when it was God who took her, was he doing the right thing? Peter, having grown up with both religious training and time travel training, didn't see it the same way and shared his point-of-view with Mig.

In the end, Mig had written the note to Carrie, and then he had asked Peter to let him think about it for a few more days. Peter had said that he would wait to hear from Mig, but after Mig left, Peter had gone right away to save Carrie. At the time, he'd told himself that it was better to do it while Mig was unsure, so if there were spiritual repercussions they would fall entirely on himself.

Peter had come to understand that his refusal to help Carrie wasn't just about Mig's letter, or his promise to Mig not to help her. It was also because Peter knew that he had taken the choice away from Mig. For that, Peter felt guilty and, in a way, his guilt had contributed to his refusing Carrie's requests as much as anything else.

In the morning, after Dr. Lopez gave Peter a thorough check up, he told Peter he didn't see any new issues. "You've survived the night, so I'll take that as a good sign," the doctor said, rolling his eyes.

Peter thanked him. Slowly he stood, holding his ribs again. The doctor asked Carrie, "Could you please take him home?"

They said their good-byes to Dr. Lopez and Carrie drove Peter back to the alley, as he insisted on retrieving his car. She waited while he got in, disliking the alley even in daylight. Then, although Peter waved her away, she followed him all the way home.

When they were parked in his driveway, he waved. "I don't need help. You head on home."

Still, she walked beside him, holding his elbow all the way up the sidewalk to his front door, and he tolerated the assistance.

Peter unlocked his door and stepped inside. Carrie asked if he needed anything.

"No, I'm all right," he insisted, his voice edged with grumpiness. "You should go, Carrie. But come back here at 8 o'clock tomorrow night. Would you do that?"

"Yes," Carrie said, "but will you tell me why?"

"Well, I'm sure you'll agree that it's not wise to let Mr. Duke keep after me — and you — any longer. Today I'm going to rest. Tomorrow I'm going to take a trip and, for that, I'd like your help. Let's get this bastard dealt with and start a new week with all of this behind us."

Carrie felt the hair stand up on the back of her neck. She wasn't sure he was in any shape to face Vincent Duke. She was also afraid of what Vincent might do, given more time. "I'll be here at 8 o'clock tomorrow night. Let's get this done."

She waved good-bye. Peter waved back, then closed his door.

Carrie drove home. Once she was locked inside, Carrie moved her laptop into the kitchen where she could keep her eyes on the front and back doors.

Not a good day, she thought. There had been many bad days since Mig died, but this one was different. Today, she was afraid. *Tomorrow, well, we'll just see.*

No cars drove by, but she jumped at every sound. Using her laptop, she reviewed what she'd found on Vincent Duke. She printed several news article and other items to show Peter.

When she reached the point that she couldn't stop yawning, she had a stack of papers ready to take with her to Peter's.

Leaving on every light in the house, she locked herself in the bedroom and climbed into bed, still in her clothes. She fell asleep as soon as she got into bed, and slept fitfully until the alarm clock sounded in the morning.

17 – Experience

Carrie raced toward Peter's house. It was almost 8 P.M., and she was not going to be late. When she pulled into the driveway, Peter appeared in her headlights, waving her forward to park under the fruit trees. As soon as she stepped out of the car, he said, "Hurry, we need to be inside."

She followed him up the sidewalk and through the front door. As he twisted the door lock and slid the dead bolt into place, Peter spoke quickly, explaining that he had formulated a plan to get rid of Vinnie — without killing him, he assured Carrie — but he conveyed a sense of urgency. He gave her a quick overview of his two-part plan — to talk to the neighbor before he hired Vinnie to sell his house, and to find a way to take Vinnie down a peg. "What did you find in your research?" he asked, as he locked his front door behind them.

She handed him the pages she'd printed, which he scanned while walking. It was a short list of headlines and announcements on Vincent Duke over the past decade. While never jailed, his methods had been questioned. Carrie had found one incident of assault from when he was young. The last page showed more than a dozen complaints against his realty office.

Peter thanked Carrie, and again apologized for drawing her into harm's way. "This guy is ruthless," Peter commented.

Carrie was afraid of Vinnie, but she knew that Peter had a ruthless side too. It had become apparent to her from his story about Brad's father. She guessed that Peter dipped into his own dark side when he needed to deal with people with very bad intentions. She was glad, knowing he had it in him to do harsh things to deal with Vinnie.

Mig had been able to handle disagreeable people, too, and she wished he was there. She knew Peter was prepared to do whatever was necessary to keep Vinnie from harming either of them, and she planned to help him however she could.

Carrie followed him, moving quickly down the stairs. She could see that Peter was still favoring one side, and wondered how much pain he was in from the beating. A considerable amount, she assumed.

He entered his office and she followed. Peter reached for the secret panel.

Suddenly, Carrie heard a loud crash — the sound of breaking glass, and the house alarm went off. Carrie turned toward the sound and saw Vinnie walking into the office from the patio, stepping over shards of the broken glass door which were all over the floor.

Seeing Vinnie come through the broken door terrified her. She looked at Peter. He rushed to stand between Carrie and Vinnie.

The next thing Carrie saw was Vinnie approaching Peter, pointing a small revolver at Peter's face. Vinnie was shaking, and the gun shook too. The little man's face was beet red and Carrie saw rage in his narrow eyes.

A tremendous grin cross Vinnie's face as he said, "You're taking me back to change things *right now*."

Peter was speaking with Vinnie, but Carrie couldn't comprehend what they were saying. She was frozen, terrified.

Then, she saw a slight movement. It took a second for her to grasp that the motion was Peter slowly inching toward the doorway. He was drawing Vinnie from the office into the hall. That broke fear's spell on her.

She focused on Peter's words as he spoke to Vinnie. Peter's voice sounded soft, soothing. "I'm going to take a trip back in time for you. We can go right now. Follow me to my specially-built time machine, Vinnie. It's just down the hall."

Carrie understood that Peter was leading Vinnie away from the time travel room, away from her, and toward the hallway bathroom she'd seen on her first visit. She needed to figure out what Peter was going to do when they got there, when Vinnie saw realized it was a trick, it would be dangerous for both of them.

Does Peter have a plan? No, he's winging it. She determined that she needed to do something while she had the chance, while Peter had this crazy man distracted.

Peter continued talking, backing up, ensuring Vinnie that he would help him, that Vinnie had won.

A moment later, Vinnie's back was to her. Peter was through the office doorway into the hall, and Vinnie was moving after him. It was as if Vinnie had forgotten she was there.

Looking around for a weapon, Carrie spotted the metal fan on Peter's desk. Quietly she moved close to the desk, cringing in expectation that Vinnie would catch her at any moment.

He didn't, but Peter had seen her. He stopped backing up and Vinnie stopped too. Carrie gingerly reached for the fan as Peter said, "Vinnie, I'll take you back in time, *now!*"

As he said *now*, Peter grabbed at Vinnie's wrist with both hands and pushed upward, the gun barrel no longer pointing at him. Vinnie growled as he tried to twist out of Peter's grip. Before he could pull free, Carrie rushed forward and brought the fan crashing onto the back of Vinnie's head. He pitched forward, knocking Peter down, and Vinnie landed on the office floor with a thump.

Carrie heard Peter sigh with relief, then groan, and she saw him stand up, gingerly holding his side. "Are you okay?" she asked.

Peter nodded and said, "Yes, I'm okay." He stepped over the immobile Vincent Duke on the floor to get to Carrie. Pulling the fan from her hand and placing it on the desk, he grabbed both her shoulders, looked straight into her eyes, and said, "You did good. Do not think about anything more than that. You did a very good thing."

Eyes wide, Carrie asked, "Did I kill him?"

Peter turned to look at Vinnie's still form. He could see the man's round chest rising with shallow breaths. He turned to face Carrie again, and his face grew stern. "No, Carrie, you did *not* kill him. He's breathing."

Peter let go of her shoulders. He stepped over Vinnie, picked up the revolver from the floor and tucked it into his waistband. Changing his mind, he pulled the gun out and threw it into a desk drawer, slamming it shut.

He said, "Carrie, I need to go back and correct this right now. Please follow me quickly."

Peter opened the secret panel and stepped inside the time travel room. "You're about to understand a lot more about time travel," he said.

"I'm sure," Carrie responded, as she entered the small room.

Peter closed the panel. Talking fast, he said, "Carrie do not leave this room."

She had no desire to go back into the office, not with Vinnie Duke sprawled on the floor. "Just go. I'll be fine," Carrie responded, her voice breaking.

"All right," he repeated. "No matter what you see--" he waved toward the video monitor, which was showing the four camera feeds, including one showing the rear sliding door shards on the patio stones, and another showing Vinnie on the office floor — "do not open the panel. It'll be hard, but...lord... get to sleep and everything will be okay. I promise it will be."

She saw Peter drop a chess piece on his shelf, repositioning several objects alongside it. "When I was at Vinnie's, he was ranting and I pocketed his rook," Peter explained. "He had an antique chess set in his living room. Like this guy ever had the patience to learn chess," Peter grunted.

Carrie wrung her hands and backed up against the wall, tripping over the blanket still on the floor. She steadied herself and quieted, so that Peter could concentrate.

Peter sat down on the wooden chair in the center of the time travel room. Carrie watched as he fiddled with the objects on the shelf a little more.

She looked toward the security monitors, and heard Peter take a deep breath. The room brightened, and Carrie turned toward Peter. With a puff, the room darkened, and Peter disappeared from the chair. A warm, pleasant smell enveloped her.

A minute passed, then two. Carrie glanced at the empty chair in the center of the time travel room, wishing she wasn't alone. She wished hard for Peter to return, knowing that he wouldn't. She tried to sleep, picturing herself waking up in her own bed.

Instead, she tossed and turned on the time travel room floor, trying to get comfortable as time passed. Checking the clock, she saw more than an hour had passed.

Suddenly, she heard noises coming from Peter's office. Looking at the video monitor, she saw a bloody-faced Vinnie peering around the room. She heard Vinnie bellow Peter's name and her heart thumped. She froze, trying not to make a sound.

Vinnie pushed everything off Peter's desk and began pulling out the drawers and dumping them. She covered her face with the blanket edge, willing herself to breathe quietly, watching the rampage happening on the other side of the wall.

Vinnie stopped. Carrie saw him pulling the gun from Peter's desk drawer. Vinnie raised it and fired once into Braggin's desk. Carrie scooted low on the floor, squeezing herself into the corner as far as she could. She heard the gun fire several more times and covered her ears. She dared look at the monitor, and saw him shooting the chair behind the desk. Vinnie knocked over the velvet chair and fired into it twice, cursing Peter.

She slowly crawled toward the panel, unsure what she'd do if she reached it. She didn't want to open it, nor go in the office with Vinnie shooting.

Then, everything fell quiet. Wondering what was going on, Carrie turned slowly, silently, to look at the video monitor. She saw Vinnie standing, swaying slightly, in front of Peter's desk. His mouth opened as if to shout and... he disappeared.

In the blink of an eye, Vinnie was gone from the room, wiped away like grime on a window. Carrie stared at the video monitor. The sliding door looked pristine. The glass was unbroken, and she could see the patio was clear. Listening, she heard only the faint chirp of a night bird from the backyard, and an electronic hum from somewhere upstairs.

It took a second for her to register what had happened. Somehow, at some time, Peter had taken care of Vincent Duke. His attack on them had never happened.

Carrie moved back to the corner of the room, relieved, her heart still pumping fast. She took a deep breath, the sweet smell in the room filling her lungs. Her thoughts drifted away, and she fell asleep.

18 – Revisions

Carrie woke up in her bed. *I slept well for being curled up in a corner.* At least, she was refreshed as if she'd slept well.

Suddenly alert, her head flooded with memories. She remembered Vinnie's first confrontation with her on the street, she and Peter meeting at the barbecue restaurant, hitting Vinnie on the head, and seeing the sliding door unbroken — though the first three memories were dream-like, less solid than the last.

She was surprised that she didn't feel weirder than she did. After all, she'd seen Peter, then Vinnie, disappear in front of her eyes the night before. As they did so often, her thoughts turned to Mig. She wanted to tell him all about her adventure, and it made her sad that he wasn't there to hear. *If Mig were here, he and I would have helped Peter together.* While it made her sad to think of what Mig was missing, she knew he'd also be happy she was knee-deep in time travel adventures.

Lost in thought, a few minutes later, Carrie heard a ping from her cell phone, alerting her to a voice mail. She picked up the phone, and listened to the message from Peter. He said it was "safe" and invited her to come to his house for coffee, "when you're ready."

She was eager for answers, dressed quickly, and jumped in the car. She needed to know what Peter had done on his trip.

***

"Good morning," Peter said as she walked in his front door. Carrie thought that he looked tired. His eyes were ringed by dark circles. He asked her, "So, what did you do yesterday?"

Carrie knew he was checking to see what she remembered. "I remember it all," Carrie assured him. "I remember Vincent Duke, how he followed me, how he grabbed me--" She stopped and looked down at her arm, checking if the bruises were still there. They weren't. *Never were*, she thought.

"Excellent," Peter said.

"I remember you telling me Mr. Duke wanted you to make him wealthier. I remember going for barbecue with you." She paused, thinking. "You know, I remember what's happened these past few days instead of all that too. I guess, I have memories of new things and old things."

Peter looked at her seriously, "You've collected more dream-like memories and solid memories."

Carrie nodded. She'd experienced a dreamy memory or two when he'd saved the horse from attack. She understood his timeline lessons so much better now, as days-worth of memories related to Vincent Duke floated wispily across her mind. She glanced at her arm again, amazed that it wasn't even tender, no bruises marking it.

He handed Carrie a mug of steaming coffee and picked up his own. She held her coffee mug aloft and said, "Here's to your time travels, Mr. B."

Peter lifted his mug and clinked it against Carrie's in response to her informal toast.

Carrie thought of the night she'd found Peter by the dumpster, now a hazy memory. She asked, "What about Dr. Lopez?"

Peter shook his head, "Our visit didn't happen, as things are now. He is not going to remember. Still, he's been my friend for some time. In fact, he has smoky memories of his own from a trip years ago. Maybe some day he and I can tell you *his* tale."

Peter rose and asked Carrie to follow him. She grabbed her coffee mug and followed him downstairs to his office.

After quizzing Carrie for a while, mixing his questions with explanations, Peter proceeded to tell Carrie about his trip into the past to deal with Vincent Duke. Peter explained that after he settled onto the chair in the time travel room, he dropped Vinnie's chess piece onto his trinket shelf — Carrie recalled seeing him do that — and then he had focused on where and when he wanted to be. He went on his trip into the past, leaving the empty chair Carrie had observed.

Where he went, he told her, was to a neighborhood party several years back, when his neighbor — the one who had hired Vinnie to sell his home — had first moved into the house next door.

"Good thing Vinnie's thug didn't mark up my face," Peter quipped.

Peter explained that in the original timeline, he had only stayed at the party long enough to say hello to everyone, show his crazy persona around a little, and wolf down a hamburger. When he traveled back in time, the time traveler version of Peter waited until he knew that the then-version of himself had left the party and gone home.

Then, his time-traveling-self sidled up to the then-new-neighbor. Peter struck up a conversation. He carefully brought up the neighbor's recent move and found that Vinnie had been the neighbor's agent for the purchase. Peter steered the conversation toward Vinnie's worst traits, assuming correctly that Vinnie had always been an ass. After a while, Peter had the neighbor convinced he'd never liked Vinnie's attitude at all.

Peter believed that what he'd done would help avoid their future problems, but his plan included much more than just removing Vinnie's chance at selling the neighbor's house. He'd sensed a shift in the timeline, and knew that the danger of the neighbor hiring Vinnie was gone.

He hadn't stopped there, though. Armed with the knowledge Carrie had given him about Vinnie's checkered past and business complaints, Peter kept chatting with his neighbor. A few drinks later, Peter got what he needed to make the second part of his plan work. The inebriated neighbor admitted that Vinnie had convinced him to pay part of the purchase under-the-table to lower the taxes. He'd saved a bundle, the neighbor told Peter. This was confirmation Peter had been seeking, and he excused himself from the party.

Peter explained to Carrie that he had guessed that with Vinnie's lust for money and power, it was likely that he had done very bad things. Peter knew there would be something, he just didn't know for sure what it would be. What she'd found had been enough to point him in the right direction: tax fraud.

Hearing from his neighbor that Vinnie had broken the rules on his real estate transaction gave Peter hoped that Vinnie had broken the rules more than once. He could use Vinnie's own actions against him, let him reap what he had sown. All Peter had to do was get the right information to the right person, and let the law take care of the rest.

So, before coming back to his own time, Peter said to Carrie that he had made one more stop. He walked downtown — a little far but it had still been early in the day — and he visited an attorney friend there.

Peter knew that his past-self had crashed on the couch after leaving the neighborhood party, so he didn't have to worry about being seen in two places. There was no chance of two Peter Braggins being seen walking around town.

Peter suggested to his attorney friend — whom Peter knew would soon be taking a job in the county District Attorney's office — that Vincent Duke might be playing fast-and-loose with some of his real estate transactions. The two men talked for a little while, his friend promising to look into Mr. Duke's activities.

Peter then left the attorney's office, concentrated, and made the trip home. He'd awaken in his bed, and left Carrie a message right away to tell her it was safe.

"And here you are," he shrugged. Then he said seriously, "I don't think he'll be bothering us anymore. I've already checked outside, and my neighbor is still moving, but he's using a different person to sell his house. Plus, articles I found online from several months ago show Vincent Duke dealing with some serious legal woes."

"Good," Carrie said, still mentally sorting the clear new memories from the hazy not-memories, and glad to be done with all the trouble this man Vinnie had been. She'd been terrified when Vinnie threatened Peter with the gun, and horrified at her actions as she'd knocked Vinnie out. Knowing that it had all been wiped away, had not happened, helped her to feel better about it.

Peter made a quick breakfast for them. The meat he'd recently served in tacos was making another appearance, this time as a burrito with eggs and potatoes. Carrie guessed that he prepared meat in advance pounds at a time, but ate it as leftovers for one, and felt pity for him.

When they'd finished eating, Peter said, "I know you vape, Carrie. Let's step outside. Believe it or not, I'm going to smoke a cigarette." He watched for her to react, grinning.

She reacted with a surprised laugh. Without a word of comment, she walked outside with him.

Sitting at the patio table, Peter offered to continue Carrie's time-travel education. After the evening's odyssey she wanted nothing but sleep. "I'd like that, but for now can I have a raincheck? It's been a wild ride, and I didn't even time travel! You must be exhausted, aren't you?"

Peter touched his ribs, and Carrie noticed he didn't wince. "I could use a little recuperation time. The wounds may have disappeared, but my spirit needs some healing time."

As she got up from the table, Carrie realized that she had a tale of her own to tell. "I think I might know something that you don't. After you disappeared from the time travel room, Vinnie trashed your office."

She saw a look of shock on Peter's face. "You're kidding," he said.

"Nope," she continued, "He shot bullets in your walls and furniture. It was quite a mess." She grinned. She couldn't help herself, as pleased as she was to have a memory that the time traveler didn't.

Peter stared at her, agape.

She grinned back.

"You mean to tell me you saw the correction happen... on the security monitor in the time travel room?"

"Yes, I did," Carrie said. "The monitors were showing Vinnie in there, and the next moment it showed your empty office."

"Unbelievable," Peter muttered. Shaking his head, he said to Carrie, "I never thought of the cameras catching a time change. Well, but I'm not here to see the monitors. I'd be off..." He rubbed his chin, and Carrie almost heard gears turning in his head.

Mumbling to himself, she overheard, "The system is inside the room, and protected, so I can understand how..."

He held his hands out, palm up and shrugged. "You know, Carrie, I've never even checked the security footage. I just put the thing in there last year because I didn't want anyone sneaking up on me when I was in there working late at night. But, I never actually considered that they might record a..." He froze.

"What's wrong?"

"That could be a problem. If the system has recorded, and the Vinnie correction is on there, I'll need to get rid of the security system. Otherwise, it is recording proof that someone — say a government agency — might find. I don't want to have proof like that sitting around. I must look into that."

He shook his head again, and stared wide-eyed at Carrie. "Well done." Carrie was surprised to see a look of pride on Peter's face. "I guess even an old dog like me can learn new things."

"Glad I could help, Peter."

Peter stabbed out his cigarette, which he'd barely smoked. "You know," he said, "I stayed in that room plenty of times when Grampa took a trip, and I can't remember a single time that I knew something that Grampa didn't."

He applauded Carrie and said, "You would make one heck of a time traveler."

Carrie smiled. She saw the pride in his eyes again. "Maybe I could," she answered.

19 – Safe

The following weekend, Carrie met Peter at the state park miles away from town. When he'd called to invite her, he had said that he wanted to be more cautious about their meeting publicly. She liked the park, and was glad to take some outdoor time.

They walked and talked. Peter did most of the talking. He seemed to enjoy sharing his stories with her, and her curiosity kept her listening. *Who could resist? It's such a good opportunity to hear a time traveler's stories?*

She took a deep breath of the pine-scented air, then let it out in a long *Ah*. "It is nice to be out-and -about," she said.

Peter cleared his throat, and in what sounded to her to be a grim tone, he said, "Carrie, I must show you something." Peter pulled a folded newspaper, the state capital area paper, from his back pocket. He unfolded it and handed it to Carrie.

The headline gave her chills, *Nash County Real Estate Agent* Killed in Police Standoff.

She bit her lip and read on. The article described the recently shamed Vincent Duke's actions the previous day.

Carrie gasped. The article outlined how police arrived at Duke's home following up on a missing person's report filed by his girlfriend Lana Brier's roommate. Apparently, Vinnie had reacted badly to the police's approach and refused to open his door.

After a brief standoff, Vincent Duke was killed. In searching the house, police found Lana's body in Mr. Duke's basement, along with her dog, which had been shut in the basement with her body.

Carrie stopped reading and stared, wide-eyed at Peter.

"Oh, keep reading," he urged.

The article next mentioned that police, in trying to notify family members, found that Mr. Duke's half-brother was missing, as were Ms. Brier's parents. Police would be searching Mr. Duke's property, his family's home, and the Briers' home, for what they feared might be more bodies.

"Wow," Carrie exclaimed.

Peter took back the newspaper. He shook his head, "We certainly knew that he was dangerous. I had no idea how far he had gone already."

Carrie suddenly had a terrible thought, "Peter, did we drive him to this?"

He put his hand on her shoulder and squeezed. "No," he said firmly. "This was his doing, not ours."

He sighed, looking toward the sky, "Maybe I went little further than I needed to in exposing his deeds. Really, though, the blame lies with Vincent Duke. He did what he did all by himself. Even in our smoky memories, before our correction he had started it. He came after us. He alone is to blame. As things are, we are not being counted among his victims."

Carrie's mouth went dry at the thought that she could have been one of Vincent Duke's victims. *How pointless would that have been?*

She hadn't seen Vinnie approaching her that day downtown, as she'd been looking at his SUV when he walked right up on her. She blew out a breath, half in relief and half in horror at what might-have-been.

Peter let go of her shoulder and continued walking along the trail. "You watch and see, Carrie, and I'll bet there are bodies on that man from even before I went back in time. He was unbalanced long before I...we met him, so..."

Carrie followed Peter down the trail. She caught up to him, and they walked along in a tense silence.

Carrie broke the silence. "So, what now?"

"Who knows," Peter said lightly.

Peter stopped, lowering himself with a grunt onto a large rock near the water. He motioned for Carrie to sit down on a nearby rock. "Old bones," he said, grinning at her.

Carrie remembered his age and wondered if he wasn't kidding. She took a seat after scanning the rock for snakes.

"I'm kidding. I'm kidding," Peter said.

Peter suddenly changed the subject, "I had a dog once."

"Oh," said Carrie, surprised at the jarring transition. "Um, that's nice. What kind?"

"Shelter dog. Kind of looked like a German Shepherd. I used to bring him to this very park." He paused. "I took a trip to help a family once. When I returned, I didn't have a dog anymore. Had never had him." He turned toward Carrie, "I embarrassed myself for a few minutes arguing with the neighbor who'd been dog-sitting, before it struck me what had happened, and I backtracked."

He paused, and Carrie saw his face change to a look of surprise, and she imagined a light bulb appearing over his head, "Come to think of it, that woman still looks at me kind of funny when she's out walking *her* dog."

Carrie didn't know how to respond to that. She wanted to laugh, but was sad for Peter, so held it in and waited for him to go on.

"While I try to be careful about the ripples that I cause, I guess I treat them a bit like a side effect that has to be tolerated. Coming back and having that ripple where I'd changed something for another person — not a relative, not a friend — and found that it had affected my seemingly-unrelated life, gave me pause. I questioned my rules and whether changes were reaching further than I thought they were."

He kicked at a rock by his foot, frowning. "Turned out that the dog I'd adopted had belonged to the daughter of people I'd taken a trip to help. The man's mother had been robbed and beaten a few days before they came to see me. The man —

Arthur — was feeling guilty because his mother had asked him to set up outdoor motion lights for her a few weeks before she was robbed, and he hadn't done it.

"Valid or not, he felt guilty and wanted me to change it so that he had helped his mother when she asked. Then, he hoped the men who had broken in would have instead been scared away by the lights, and she could avoided being beaten.

"When I changed their circumstances, it turned out not only did the break-in never happen, but another thing that didn't happen was that their daughter's dog hadn't run away and ended up at the shelter. It had run away while they were all at the hospital. So, when the woman didn't end up in the hospital, my dog — the daughter's dog, I mean — never ran away, and so he was never at the shelter for me to adopt.

"It's funny, though, that with all I — and Grampa — have adjusted this timeline for humans, and all the ripple effects that we deemed to be safe, it took the impact of my time changes on an old German Shepherd mix for me to slow down and take stock of the impact I had. It certainly affected my life," Peter continued. "It confirmed to me the folly of trying to have even a pet — forget any idea of having a wife, or a family, with my travels potentially impacting them negatively.

"Your Grampa had a family," Carrie said.

He smiled at Carrie. "Obviously, he had my mother. But, I can never convince myself that my doing so would be prudent, and when I lost that dog, I took it as proof that I'd made the right choice."

Peter sighed. "I still miss that dog. I'd named him Max. It turned out his name was *Rex*. Surprisingly close," he mused. His brow furrowed.

"It's not too late," Carrie chimed, trying to sound positive. "You could get another dog..." She trailed off. No argument she made could possibly be a match for his years of logical thought thinking and his time travel experience.

Peter looked at Carrie. His expression relaxed, and he appeared amused, "Thank you. But, I am beginning to think that the consequences could be more serious than I originally thought. It's just not a chance I'm going to take."

Peter stopped talking and looked out over the water. The two of them sat silently for a while, listening to the water lapping, birds calling, and far-off human voices.

"Well, I'm ready to go. Thank you for coming out to meet me." Peter let out a long breath. "I just wanted you to know that we have nothing more to fear from Vincent Duke."

He looked her in the eye, "And I wanted to thank you for helping. Well done."

"It was an honor," Carrie said, and she meant it.

Peter said good-bye to Carrie in the parking lot, then turned and walked up the trail toward the far parking lot where he'd parked. She'd offered to drive him to his car, but Peter said, "I can get there on my own, thank you."

She didn't leave the park right away. Carrie watched as Peter walked the trail, at times going out of sight when the trail curved. She saw him stoop once, picking up something — she couldn't see what. He straighten, and whatever he'd grabbed he dropped into his pocket.

She watched him for a few minutes, then set off for the drive home.

20 – Holiday

Carrie was wide awake as the clock crept over midnight and Easter Sunday arrived. The kids would be arriving in the morning. She looked forward to it, and felt sad at the same time.

For the past few weeks, Carrie had been caught up in learning about time travel and helping Peter. It had been distracting her from her grief, though Mig was always in her thoughts. Lying in the dark now, there was no distraction and her head was filled with Easter memories. She closed her eyes and let them drift through her mind. Then came the memories of other holidays when Mig was with them.

She tried to focus on the joy of the coming Easter day, but her heart still felt broken to pieces. It was going to be hard seeing the grandchildren digging through their Easter baskets without Mig there to joke with them and pretend to eat their candy.

Carrie watched the ceiling fan spin in the faint light spilling in from the kitchen, where she had left the light on. She knew today's holiday meal would be a celebration but also sad, with the kids and grand-kids remembering and crying. She worried the day might be more than she could bear. She began to cry at the thought of not just having a hard day, but not having Mig there to share in the joyful moments.

She said aloud, "I wish you were here with all of us, Mig." Twenty minutes later, curled up in bed, eyes red, from crying, she stared at the clock.

***

When her alarm went off early in the morning, Carrie forced herself out of bed, made coffee, and pushed her sad thoughts to the back of her mind. There were preparations to be made for the family holiday dinner.

She busied herself cleaning things, making sure the house was in good shape for the coming visitors. Cleaning allowed her to focus on the broom or the rag rather than thinking too deeply. She didn't want thoughts of Vincent Duke to ruin the day.

Since the kids had moved out on their own, whenever they came to visit, she wanted the house to be tidy and clutter-free. When the youngest were still living at home, Carrie remembered that it seemed like there was always clutter: school papers on the table, dirty clothes piled in the laundry room, and half-eaten food on plates abandoned on the kitchen counter. She saw the house tidiness now and missed the messiness of the four of them together in the house.

She found herself thinking that Mig was with her, surveying the tidied house, and would be watching over the family today. That thought gave her comfort, and she smiled.

Just as Carrie finished straightening the living room furniture, her cell phone rang. It was her sister, Kim, calling to wish her a happy Easter. Carrie returned the wish. They talked briefly. Just as Carrie was preparing for her kids to arrive, Kim was preparing for her grown children, too. They ended the call, and Carrie headed to the kitchen to double-check the meal's ingredients were all ready.

The kids and grandchildren poured in the door after noon. First came her stepdaughter, Nicole, with her husband Greg and the three grandchildren.

Carrie brought out their Easter baskets and lined them up, each labeled with a name. She had even put out candy bars for the grown-up kids.

Carrie put a ham in the oven. They all worked together preparing the potatoes, beans, and desserts. She and the kids laughed and cried as they cooked. *Smiles and cries*, Carrie heard Mig say in her head.

The rest of the kids arrived within minutes of each other. The oldest, Juli with her husband, Corvi. Then, Carrie's son Dylan and his girlfriend Brianna, followed by the youngest, Grace. All pitched in, and each had added a side dish or dessert to the growing feast.

Mig's father, whom Mig had always called Pop, came in a little while later and Carrie greeted him with, "Hey, Pop," just as Mig would have.

When everyone she was expecting had arrived, Carrie called them all to the table. It was filled: a steaming half-carved ham sat in the center, surrounded by sweet potatoes, mashed potatoes, salad, broccoli, and other side dishes. Together they had created a beautiful meal to share.

One of the grandchildren had set an extra place setting at the head of the table, where Mig would have been sitting. Before Dylan could say grace, they all broke down crying.

Just as Thanksgiving and Christmas had been difficult with Mig's absence, this first Easter dinner was too. It was several minutes before everyone settled themselves, then Dylan said the blessing and began passing plates of food around the table.

Carrie took one of the bread rolls and passed the plate. She slathered butter on the roll. Normally, this would be one of her holiday favorites. Like so many things since Mig's death, though, the roll's taste was muted and unexciting. She ate to sustain life, as Mig would have said, but nothing tasted as delicious as it used to taste.

The family chatted as they passed the food around the table. They caught Carrie up on their lives as they shared stories of what they'd been doing, plans that they were making, and they all shared memories of Mig.

Dylan broke the news that his longtime girlfriend was now his fiancé. They would be marrying in the summer. Carrie cried from happiness, and they all cried that Mig wouldn't be there to see it; at least not in body, only in spirit.

Their youngest daughter Grace — technically Mig's stepdaughter — was settling in for her first year at a college away from home.

The oldest daughters — Mig's daughter Nicole and Carrie's oldest Juli — brought her up-to-speed with their busy, adult lives.

From time-to-time, the grandchildren chimed in with stories of high school and college. Carrie still couldn't believe one of the *grandchildren* was in college, as was Grace. She wished so hard that Mig was there to share it all with them. Carrie felt the happiest she'd felt in months.

Pop told a story about his mother. He talked about his mother cooking for the holidays, then talked about when he was young and harvested sugar beets. He ended with a story about Mig as a little boy checking his Easter basket. The last left everyone teary-eyed.

For dessert, Juli had made a pecan pie using Carrie's mother's recipe. It was delicious. Everyone chatted, laughed, and savored their pieces of pie.

After dessert, the family ventured outside. It was a warm afternoon. Carrie vaped, then took candid photos while the family chatted and walked around. Her photographs were never as good as Mig's, but since he wasn't there, she took it as her duty to make a record of the day.

Suddenly, she remembered that she wasn't supposed to be there. She wouldn't be, except that Mig had saved her from the car accident. Though he hadn't known it would work out the way it did, he'd kept the kids from being orphans now. She determined to make the most of the day and take a lot more photos. She clicked away.

Mig and the kids built a patio out back and they'd set the telescope and lawn chairs on it. On cool evenings, they'd bundle in their coats and watch their breath as Mig brought celestial objects into view. She could picture Mig, carefully finding celestial objects and then letting each of them look. He chose stars, planets, the moon, and directed the telescope, refocusing by hand when he found his target.

Once he had an object in sight, he'd bring each of them up to look at it. They took turns, Carrie and the two youngest children, as Mig showed them the universe.

Her daughter tapped her on the arm, startling Carrie out of her thoughts. "It's a nice night, Mom. Can we bring out Dad's telescope?" Grace asked.

Carrie was glad that she wasn't the only one remembering the fun nights outside with Mig. Carrie nodded and said, "That sounds like a good idea."

Dylan and Greg carried the telescope outside. The kids took turns looking through the telescope at the moon and stars, showing the grandchildren these far-off objects. Greg Junior, the youngest of the pack, exclaimed at the wonder of the close-up moon.

They stayed outside for a long while, taking turns looking through the eyepiece. Carrie took more photographs, despite the low light. When the wind picked up and gusts became more frequent, Dylan scooped up the telescope and they all headed inside for leftovers.

When they departed that evening, everyone hugged and talked about plans to get together again soon.

Peter awoke Easter morning to find a basket of candy on his bedside table. He bolted upright, and ran down the stairs to the sound of the coffee maker brewing and silverware jangling.

Alfonso Horacio turned and greeted Peter warmly as he entered the kitchen.

"Well, mijo. Now that your recent adventure is behind you, I thought we might have that talk you wanted."

Peter wrapped his grandfather in a hug, shaking his head at the old man's ability to know what was happening without asking. He'd thought he'd grown used to it decades ago, but he still marveled at how much his Grampa could discern from the future.

Over coffee and a hearty breakfast, Alfonso shared stories of his life in the future, which was pleasant yet lonely. Coming to see Peter had tired him, as would returning, but he was pleased for the opportunity for them to spend the day together. "I especially am happy to have eggs again. We don't have them *when* I am."

When Peter looked aghast, Alfonso laughed until he cried. "I'm kidding, mijo. Just teasing you."

When his Grampa had finally stopped chuckling over his joke, Peter filled in the gaps of his Grampa's knowledge of his life. There was little to talk about personally; everything he shared centered on time travel, including background on the Vincent Duke saga not mentioned in newspapers, his "student" Carrie, and her departed husband.

When Peter filled his plate with a second helping of eggs, his Grampa declining, Alfonso startled him by saying, "I broke a promise to your grandmother."

Peter avoided dropping his plate and returned quickly to his seat at the counter. "Tell me." He couldn't fathom that his Grampa, who had instilled in him that his word was his bond, had at some point broken his word.

"When your mama became pregnant with Simon, she stopped time traveling. I think you know this, yes?"

"Yes."

"Well, your Grandma had allowed me to travel with your mama Renee since she was a child. But, when Renee announced that she was pregnant, she stopped. Soon after, your grandmother told me how much it had scared her to travel with me. She had done so just once, back around the time we married. I knew she didn't like it and never went again. But, until she told me how much it had frightened her, I'd had no idea. After telling me of her traumatic feelings, my wife asked me not to tell our soon-to-be-born grandchild, nor any future grandchildren, about time travel. She said that I must promise to leave it to our daughter to decide for her children. And I promised her I would."

"But you did tell me. That's the promise you broke?"

Alfonso continued, sounding flustered. "That was before our first grandchild had been born, and I promised, yes, but how could I know what being a grandfather would be like? I told your older brother Simon when he turned 18, and your mother still hadn't said anything to him. The promise was already broken before I told you, too."

Peter pushed his eggs around on his plate. He hadn't known that his Grandma had ever traveled, nor that Simon knew about time travel. Then again, Simon had died at 18, so there had been little time to tell his younger brother, presumably. "What did Grandma say when she found out that you had told Simon?"

Resting his chin in his hand, his Grampa's expression grew grim, then brightened. "Your Grandma didn't find out until long after I told you, and was very, very angry with me for breaking my promise. But, after she yelled at me a while, she said that she understood and forgave me. That was a nice surprise!"

"She forgave you? Just like that?" From what Peter knew of his grandmother, that didn't sound like her at all. She'd been a brusque woman much of the time, though in the years before she died, she had becoming doting and spent an inordinate amount of time teaching Peter her favorite recipes.

Alfonso put his plate in the sink, refilled his mug with coffee, and moved his tall chair at the counter closer to Peter. "Can you imagine if I had not broken my promise to her, P.H.?

If I had not told you, or Simon, what your own mother would not tell you? Time travel, you took to like a duck to water. You had acted responsibly in letting your brother go to rest. That is why she said she forgave me: because you were a natural."

"So, you're saying it was okay to break your promise, did I get that right?" A perturbed Peter found himself rethinking his grandfather's ethics in the back of his mind. It was as if a spring had sprung loose and gears were whirring in there.

Clasping Peter's shoulder, Alfonso said, "With time travel, you made the world better. With my help, of course," Alfonso chuckled. Then, he asked, "So, P.H., does keeping your promise to Mig Weathers make the world better, or worse?"

21 – Sun and Sand

The Monday after Easter, the house feeling far too quiet, Carrie decided to give the beach another try. The weather was warming, and she knew that it was the kind of day when Mig would want to go fishing. She wanted to feel close to her husband by doing something that they had both loved to do, and decided that she was ready to fish again.

Carrie drove a circuitous route to the beach. She stopped at a farm stand and picked up strawberries for a snack. Later, she pulled into a gas station and wandered around inside, grabbing some of their favorite travel and beach snacks.

She even remembered to buy sunscreen.

This drive to the beach was different from when she'd come for the first time without Mig and the kids. Then, she'd been upset at every turn. Now, as she drove past familiar places, she found joy at the memories. There was still sadness, but the good memories won the day.

When she arrived at Topsail Island and stepped onto the pier, she felt worlds better. She loved to fish. Carrie and Mig's mutual enjoyment of catching their dinner was one of the many things that they had — used to have, she corrected herself — in common.

Memories flooded into her mind. As she rented a fishing pole and bought bait, she recalled Mig standing next to her doing the same things, at the same rental counter, many times.

Once she'd paid for everything, she walked onto the pier for the first time alone. She felt Mig walking beside her as he had done so many times, and tears of happiness leaked from her eyes.

Her heart panged, grief rearing its head. Distracted momentarily, she bumped the fishing rod's end against a picnic bench. The jolt brought her into the moment and she straightened her loads, wiping her cheeks quickly, hoping no one had seen her crying. The last thing that she needed was someone asking her if she was all right; she knew she'd break down completely.

Carrie straightened and walked with purpose down the pier. She breathed in the salt air deeply and smiled at resurrected memories of Mig fishing with her.

Halfway down the pier where the water deepened, past the swimmers, others had their lines in the water. She set everything down on an empty bench. She thought to turn and ask Mig if this bench was a good spot, stopping herself before she spoke out loud and drew attention. Her heart fell, but she didn't cry. *Progress.*

Listening to the waves and wind, Carrie cast out her line. As it hit the water, she put everything else out of her mind. The pier, and the fond memories it brought to mind, washed negative thoughts away in moments.

The peace, clearing of the mind, and relaxing focus of watching the line ride the waves put her at ease. The sun shone, and light clouds floated by. She dug the tube of sunscreen out of her bag and slathered it on her face and arms.

She'd been fishing for an hour when she noticed a man setting up a dozen feet down the pier. He threw down his gear noisily and commented aloud to himself as he set up. Carrie focused on her line and tried to ignore his annoying and obvious plea for attention.

Her fishing rod twitched. She picked up the rod and watched the line for the next twitch, prepared to set the hook.

She could hear the annoying fisherman yelling, "You got a bite! Get it!" She already had the pole in her hand. In her head only, she told the man, *Shut up. I know.*

He kept blathering, Carrie ignoring him and doing what she needed to do. He came closer and yelled, "Set that hook now!"

I know what to do, damn it, she thought. The line twitched, and she jerked the pole. Seconds later, she felt the familiar tug and knew she had a fish on her line. She began reeling.

"Reel it in! Reel it in!" the annoying man yelled.

"I'm all set," she said. "Thank you." She made herself sound friendly, barely. *Another problem of fishing without Mig,* she thought, *is men think I need their help. Then again, that's any time I went somewhere without Mig.*

He kept barking instructions at her anyway. *I don't even know you,* Carrie thought to herself. "I'm all set," she said aloud, hoping he'd take the hint.

She tried to focus on the fish and her line, blocking out his voice as best she could. She reeled and felt what might be a sizeable fish fighting her. It took her a minute to get it onto the pier. *That was fun,* she thought, as she carefully removed the hook from a 12-inch sea trout.

All the time, the fisherman kept talking, almost barking orders. She hated how patronizing he sounded. As she let the fish go, he balked, "Oh! That was a nice one. Why'd you let that go? I'd have taken it!"

"I'm catching and releasing, sorry." She grabbed a shrimp and started baiting her line. The man was still muttering; she tried to ignore the sound.

She cast out over the waves, trying to focus on the natural sounds around her. Her peaceful mood was being replaced by annoyance and she tried to relax again.

She tried.

The annoying man kept approaching Carrie, trying to make conversation, asking to "borrow" things, and in general disturbing her peace. She knew if Mig was here, he'd take care of the guy, gently but firmly. *But he isn't, so it's all on me*, Carrie thought angrily.

"Be nice," she heard Mig say in her head. He took the high road, except for rare situations when "nice" wasn't enough. Carrie thought this was one such situation.

She closed her eyes and focused on the warmth of the breeze blowing across the pier. She took a few deep breaths and opened her eyes, watching her line with intense scrutiny, waiting for the next nibble.

No matter how much she concentrated, though, she could still hear the attention-seeker walking around talking about the fish he'd caught and asking everyone what they'd caught. She heard him belittling the sizeable fish that another person nearby had reeled in.

One woman he approached told the man to look in her bucket at the five-pounder she'd landed. The man made a snide comment Carrie couldn't hear, then she heard him muttering angrily as he went back to his own spot. She looked over and the woman, who saw Carrie looking and pointed at the man's retreating back, rolling her eyes. Carrie grinned and nodded in response.

How much am I going to take from this jerk, Carrie thought to herself. She mused whether the guy would leave the pier under his own power or if someone was going to toss him over the railing into the water.

She steeled herself as she saw the fisherman approaching again. She knew she needed to be firm right now, or he was not going to quit. *Mig, you're not here but I know you have my back. Let's do this*. She braced herself for the coming exchange, and her insecurities fell away.

The fisherman asked, "Can I borrow some bait--"

"No," Carrie cut him off, not smiling this time and a little louder than she'd planned. She looked out over the water and reeled slowly, ignoring the shocked look she knew was on his face.

He walked away, muttering under his breath. She didn't give him bait, and he started to sound angry.

Carrie didn't care. He'd just come from buying hooks and didn't get himself bait, so no way would she give him any. She wanted to be done with him.

He turned toward Carrie, "All I need is a couple'a shrimp--" he started, and she cut him off.

"Buy your own!" she said loudly. *Not nice*, she thought.

But it worked. A moment later, Carrie saw him packing up his gear. He moved further down the pier, away from her. She breathed a sigh of relief.

She heard some of the others fishing around her make whispered comments thanking God for the man's departure.

Able to relax again, Carrie went on fishing. The day was bright and the air warm, and she let pleasant memories float through her mind like birds riding a breeze. Carrie enjoyed the breeze, the salty smells, and watching her line, even when the fish came few and far between.

Mid-afternoon her skin was looking a little pink. She slathered on more sunscreen, then decided to leave the pier, and spend time at the water's edge.

She gathered her gear to return to the rental counter. On the way, she stopped and gave the woman who'd rolled her eyes earlier the bait Carrie had left over. The woman thanked her.

The waves pummeled the sand as Carrie dropped her beach chair at the water's edge. She sat on the beach chair with her feet in the water. The waves covered her feet and withdrew, covered and withdrew. She closed her eyes and felt the warm water moving and the sun on her face. The water spray left a salty scent in the air. She breathed deeply and relaxed.

How hard it was to be there without Mig. She thought again that Peter's promise to Mig couldn't be the right thing. Then, Carrie thought of how she had stood up to the annoying fisherman, how Mig had almost seemed to be with her. She didn't like being without her husband, but might be able to handle whatever life threw at her. Might be able to let him rest.

In the end, she was back at the same place. She believed that she should honor Mig's wishes. *And,* she thought, *I think it's time that I tell Peter that I don't hold it against him for keeping his promise. Maybe it is time.*

Carrie stayed on the beach, occasionally retreating up the sand as the tide advanced, until she left for home.

When she woke up early the next morning, Carrie felt refreshed. It was as if her grief had cracked and opened a space where a few happier moments might squeeze in. Carrie guessed that this was probably the same as other widows or widowers experienced, when the constant hurt gave way enough to draw forth sweet remembrances, and open up for new experiences.

She'd shared that amazing man's life and every second was a gift. Moving forward, she would keep that foremost in her mind, and try more often to think of the good times, as she allowed herself to enjoy new things.

The heart wrenching pain would never be gone, it could rise at any moment, but maybe there could be shorter moments of agony and more room for joy.

And maybe, room for time travel adventures. *Mig would totally approve.*

After she filled her coffee mug, she picked up her cell phone and punched in Mr. Braggin's number. He answered right away.

"Hi, Peter, it's Carrie," she said. "I've been thinking about it and I feel like I understand why Mig left that letter with you." She felt her eyes start to tear up and steadied her voice, hoping he wouldn't know she was crying.

She continued, "I know you won't — I mean can't — make *that* correction for me, and I just wanted to tell you that I think I can be at peace with that now, with Mig's wishes and your promise. And hope we can continue talking."

"Carrie, I'm glad to hear this."

She said good-bye and ended the call before Peter could say anything more.

Tears streamed from her eyes. She let them roll and let herself cry, as she refilled her coffee and topped off Mig's untouched mug.

22 – Do Over

Peter Braggin sat at his desk, absentmindedly snapping matchsticks in half and dropping the pieces onto the desk. He had quite a pile going.

He was so tired; more than that, he was frustrated.

He snapped another match in half and dropped it onto the pile. Though he didn't know it for sure, experience told him that Carrie was probably still crying. She'd tried to hide it on the phone, but he could tell.

Grief was an emotional roller coaster, as he knew from his own experience. He'd seen Carrie's ups and downs over the past months and knew that he had the power to stop the crazy ride for her. She had been getting better but was not whole. Would likely never be whole. He thought to himself, *So many tears.*

He thought about Carrie asking for a raincheck. The idea of a break sounded good to him, too. Not just a few days, though. Maybe it was time for him to take a step back, stop traveling, and focus on his research. Or, on adding milestones to his own life.

After the decades of traveling — his entire adult life, really -- focusing on something else sounded good. Maybe he should think being alone for all the decades he had ahead of him. He liked the idea that he could find a love like Mig and Carrie's.

Until spending time with Mig and then Carrie, Peter hadn't realized how lonely he was. His house was often too quiet. He stayed busy, traveling for people and their miscellaneous problems, to keep his mind active, and avoid looking at his own problems.

He snapped another match in half, as he listened to the creaking of his big, empty house.

Peter knew that he had to accept the part he'd played in Carrie's continuing grief. He'd come to admire Carrie. Selfishly, he had enjoyed sharing his knowledge — and taking trips — with another person's help. And, he had admired Mig. Watching Mig's widow struggle instead of helping her had been difficult for him. Yes, he'd shared his secrets and eased her into time travel, given her purpose.

"It was always a tough situation," he muttered.

Yes, she deserved a correction — as much as he'd thought that Mig had deserved one when Carrie died. *But breaking my promise?*

Making the promise was a mistake. At this thought, he acknowledged that he'd made another mistake, and she was suffering — not just from Mig's promise but from Peter's guilt. His grandfather had said as much on his visit.

As Peter told his tale of woe, of the promise made, how keeping it was causing Carrie pain, his Grampa had not chastised him, but instead admitted to breaking a promise, and it worked out very well.

Impulsively, Peter decided. He would correct the timeline so that Mig could find the cancer early and, hopefully, survive it. Out loud to the empty office, he said, "This is what we do, Grampa, right?"

Peter decided not to tell Carrie what he was going to do. If he accomplished what he had in mind, she'd have no memories of him beyond the expo, so there was no need to say good-bye. This last thought saddened him most. Carrie wouldn't remember, he knew, but he would.

***

Peter worked in his office the rest of the day. He read through his interview of Carrie, circling some of his notes. Between bites of food, he sketched out a timeline with notations of years and dates.

Looking up Mig's obituary, Peter added to his sketch the date he'd died. From something Carrie had once said, about Mig fighting the cancer for 20 months, Peter knew his best chance for catching Mig's illness early was to travel back several years; likely, all the way back to the Expo where they'd first met.

He carefully chose what he should say to Mig about a possible health issue, knowing they would be meeting for the first time that day.

Finally, Peter read up on symptoms, just in case any might be visible — though he didn't have to be able to see the disease growing within Mig; he just needed to plant the idea in past-Mig's head, so that he would go see a doctor.

It was almost midnight when Peter decided that his plan was ready. He got up from the desk and scooped up the pile of notes.

Peter Braggin walked into his time-travel room. He tossed the notes in a manila folder and pulled a piece of blank paper from the cabinet. Standing, he wrote a note to himself detailing what he planned to correct. When he finished the note, he tossed it on the copier and made two copies. If all went as he planned, he might see them again someday, together. Maybe someday he'd show this note to both of them. He liked that idea.

And besides, he would have the time.

Peter Braggin sat in the wooden chair centered in the room. Picking up several small objects on a shelf beside him, he placed them as he wanted, closing one inside his fist. Then, he closed his eyes, concentrated, and vanished within the twinkling blackness.

23 – Coffee Time

Carrie woke up and stretched her arm over Mig's back, squeezing him in a half-hug.

"Good morning," Mig said. He turned to face her, and they kissed. "I'm ready for coffee." He flipped the blankets over her head and climbed out of bed, chuckling.

She tossed the blankets off and giggled. "I'll make the coffee today." Carrie slipped past him, making her way into the kitchen.

Mig smiled, said good morning again and kissed her as she walked by him. She hugged him tight to her, feeling him squeeze her in return.

They had always been close and affectionate, but since Mig's cancer scare and surgery, they both made sure that they savored more moments, and spent more time together and with their family. They both knew how lucky they were.

After pouring coffee, they sat on the couch watching the morning news and chatting about their plans for the day.

Mig asked Carrie about their article on a UFO meeting they'd attended together the night before. She picked up her laptop, checked the article online, and said, "It's on the website now under Local News and..." she switched to a different screen. "Looks like a few dozen people are reading it right now."

"Kewl," Mig said, then leaned over to give her another kiss. "Hey, do you want to go to the beach for the weekend?"

Carrie grinned. "I'd love that. We should be able to leave pretty soon, if you want. I just have this one article to finish... I still can't believe that Peter Braggin time travel guy called us with that strange story. That expo where we met him was years ago. Kind of odd that he lives in a haunted house. How weird is life?"

"Yeah," Mig said, "Glad he thought of us after all this time. You know, if he hadn't told me I looked sick back when we were interviewing him, I might not have gone to the doctor soon enough."

Carrie wrapped her hand over his. "We owe him a lot for making that comment. I'm glad you let him know how he helped you."

Mig nodded. "Yeah, glad we saw him again, and, wow, those photos I took in his office sure did come out with a weird glow. Strangest, ghostliest photos I've ever taken."

Carrie began typing on her keyboard, "Wanna round up the kids? As soon as I post this, we can load up the car."

"Good," Mig said, "I'll text and invite them now."

Epilogue

Miles away, Spiky Hair Guy sat at his computer, looking at the article Carrie had posted. He wasn't reading it; he was looking at one of the article's photos. The caption read, *Carrie Weathers with Haunted House Owner, Peter Braggin. Photo by Miguel Weathers.*

He smiled and nodded his head, then he heard a knock on his front door. A friend who worked with the coroner's office had called that morning, and he expecting it was them at the door.

"Time to go to work," he said to himself, and a wry smile crossed his lips. He chuckled at his own word-play as he went to answer the door.

About the Author

K. F. Whatley's professional writing experience spans twenty years. Starting her journey authoring nonfiction desktop publishing books, then moving into news reporting, she dove into fiction in 2006 — picking up where her teen self had left off.

After publishing short items in local literary journals, she made the leap with publication of her first novel in 2018.

Based in Eastern North Carolina, with ocean in one direction and foothills in the other, she fills her time with writing for work and pleasure, family gatherings, gardening, and trying not to trip over house cats.